O S I R I S

PUBLISHED BY DUNN BOOKS. FIRST EDITION
SEPTEMBER 2017. THIS TITLE IS ALSO AVAILABLE AS A
DUNN BOOKS EBOOK.

LIBRARY OF CONGRESS CATALOGING-IN-PUBLICATION
DATA IS ON FILE WITH THE U.S. COPYRIGHT OFFICE.

HARDCOVER: ISBN 978-0-9962352-3-5

PAPERBACK: ISBN 978-0-9962352-2-8

EBOOK: ISBN 978-0-9962352-4-2

DESIGNED BY ARCHIE FERGUSON.

MAPS BY MICHAEL NEWHOUSE.

MANUFACTURED IN THE UNITED STATES OF AMERICA.

OSIRIS

A NOVEL

ERIC C. ANDERSON

ꝺb

DUNN BOOKS

For Jim and Audrey, my parents ...

Someday I hope to offer similar inspiration and wisdom

In individuals, insanity is rare; but in groups, parties, nations and epochs, it is the rule.

—FRIEDRICH NIETZSCHE
Beyond Good and Evil

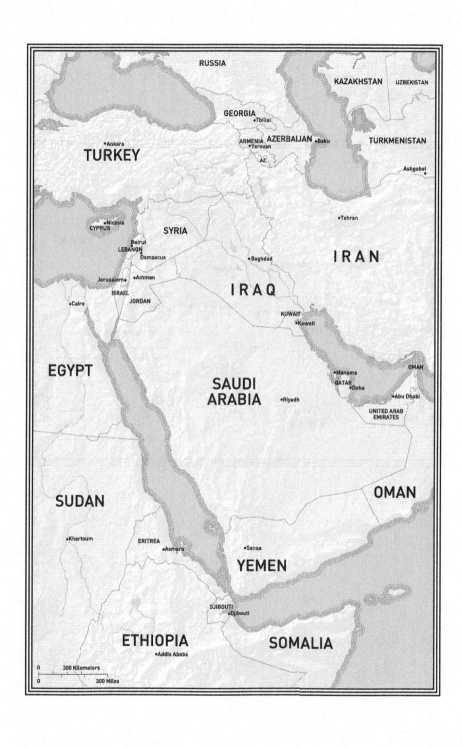

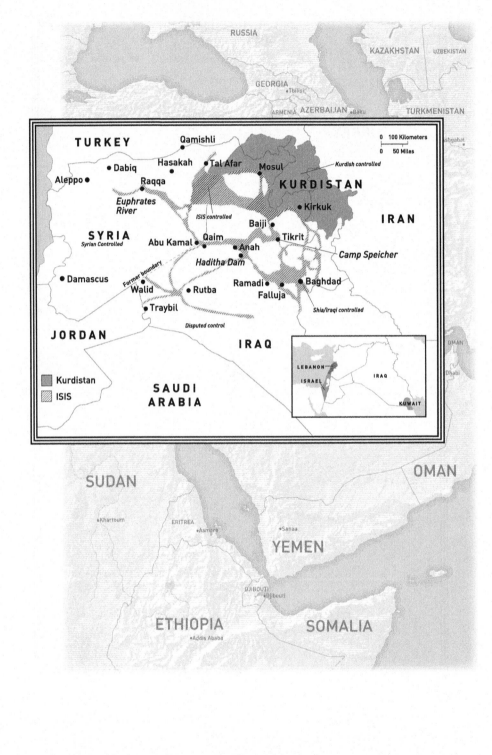

OSIRIS

PROLOGUE

RED TALCUM POWDER.

That was the only way to think about the dust storm blowing over what had once been Camp Speicher.

In movies, dust storms depicted in the Sahara Desert featured large sand dunes that covered whole camel caravans for generations to come. The sky went black, the lonely remote landscape siphoned water from your system with every breath. It was the stuff of fiction, Lawrence of Arabia. Survival always depended on finding an isolated, untouched pool of crystal-clear water.

There had been no such oasis in the bleak moonscape that confronted the first American QRF units that arrived on-scene that Sunday morning. Many of those in the lead SOF element had once called Speicher home some nearly two decades earlier.

Speicher had been ops central. Motor pools hummed with troops and contractors keeping the up-armored vehicles on the road 24/7 despite sandstorms and IEDs. The communications center was state-of-the-art, the base gym superior to those found in most American cities. Dinner was served around the clock, as was breakfast. Lunch meant sampling something between the other two options. The roads were smoothly paved so that the base commander could be driven to work each morning with a full coffee cup and not worry about spilling on his lap or, worse, onto that day's intelligence briefing. In many senses this was civilization for the U.S. military, only occasionally stained by CIA operatives, or locals claiming to be proficient translators, who all too often turned out to have other, more violent talents.

But through it all, Speicher had functioned as a bastion of American power in central Iraq for a decade.

Right up to the moment America left.

The ceremony was picture-perfect; a U.S. Army two-star handing an oversized key to a newly-minted Iraqi general. Along with $20 billion in training and American military equipment, which somehow didn't fit in the frame.

The Iraqis were granted title to hundreds of Humvees, a similar number of M1A1 Abrams main battle tanks, and a mountain of ammunition and spare parts. Washington had simply added water and boiled up an armed force it claimed (publicly and repeatedly) capable of defending borders left over from World War I. Stripped of its Sunni dictator, Baghdad now presided over a new Shia democracy, 30 million strong.

Until last Sunday.

The first bad sign had come 10 days before, when a twice-weekly logistics supply run failed to arrive as scheduled.

A second came at the end of that day, when the local security patrols failed to return to the base.

The base commander dismissed this as simple desertion, periodic jitters, nothing unusual for this volatile part of the world.

His counterpart—a realist with a Western education—was far more pessimistic.

"They're not coming back," was all he would say during each morning slideshow. (Yes, PowerPoint still ruled the day in the Iraqi military after the handover; blame the fucking Americans.)

Regardless, morale deteriorated rapidly. Morning roll call line-ups showed gaping holes in attendance. The ranks were being bled by deserters fleeing to the capital, or else back to their tribal home-towns. Uniforms lay scattered across a trash-strewn landscape outside the barbed wire perimeter.

The week clearly did not bode well for Speicher's new owners.

The end came that Sunday morning.

ISIS unveiled the revolution as a 10-truck parade, all purloined U.S. military equipment that resident Iraqi forces at first thought were their own. Drivers one, two, three and four cleared the security gate before posted guards realized something was wrong—not their fault the damn Americans figured Washington would be better served fiscally by leaving used military vehicles behind, rather than pay shipping costs. The first truck exploded in front of a gleaming command post, which completely disappeared. All four flag officers on base were dead within the first 60 seconds of the assault.

Truck Two targeted a fuel depot. The explosion was so large it set off secondary blasts at an adjacent motor pool. The third truck hit an ammunition depot, which had been placed in hardened arches, but the guards were still soft targets. The ensuing explosion cleared the way for what followed.

Truck Four was not a suicide bomb. The men who rolled out of the back killed all the remaining guards in less than five minutes, enough time for trucks Five through Ten to roll into the compound. The ISF (aka Iraqi Army) ran, like scalded cats. Those who tried to surrender were subsequently dispatched with a single shot to the head.

Not murder—revolution. A fine line between the two, but murderers do not run a flag up a ceremonial pole and then seek to govern the conquered.

Trucks Five through Ten now rolled into the compound. And with them the crazed 20-year-old foreign fighters who were willing to risk all for glory. This was not a not a pretty battle—George Custer at Little Bighorn. "Friendly fire" it was not. Both sides shot their own, by accident and on purpose.

Cries of "Allah Akbar" were already ringing out when the first air strike swept in. Death from above.

Drafted into service under an American administration that had vowed to avoid further conflict in the Middle East, the U.S. Navy and Air Force demonstrated an ability to pick off vehicles in the desert with an aplomb that scared the shit out of most ISIS commanders.

The trucks now entering Speicher had been ordered to travel without overt escort. ISIS loyalists—particularly the die-hard jihadists—only massed in urban centers where "collateral damage" precluded U.S. drone strikes. No senior ISIS member was foolish enough to use a cell phone ... and most spent time soliciting survival advice from their counterparts in Yemen and Mali.

Silence, at least electronic silence, meant another day in the trenches. Get stupid and call home ... well, you still qualified as a martyr. A dumb martyr, but still a martyr.

Speicher's raiders fell into the former category. In their haste to set up the raid, they had gone cellular. iPhone 6 was a sexy means of communication, and very vulnerable to overhead collection. The spies at NSA passed data as fast as it could be processed. "Push" close air support was launched before the final trucks even arrived at the front gate. But 300 miles of transit time still meant a lost hour. That was all it took for Speicher to become a smoking cemetery for the ISF.

Then the dust blew in.

Drone operators were the first to abandon station. Gusts from the west that drew grit up from ground zero to 15,000 feet bespoke disaster for their flimsy airframes. The drones fled for airstrips in Jordan and an unnamed facility in southern Syria. Now the aircrews were left to work with the "mark-one eyeball" and on-board imaging capabilities.

National overhead systems were next. The dust rendered electro-optical collection useless, persistent infrared quickly followed, and no one wanted to rely on radar when trying to do close air support for allies who had no radio connectivity with U.S. pilots.

An AC-130 went off target shortly after the drones. With open firing ports, the Hercules was a vacuum for this red talcum shit. Crews had learned that it almost instantly began degrading well-oiled weapons' slides and would shut down hard drives and electronic ports, including headphone plugs, within 30 minutes of inundation. A sense of humor for dealing with this crap was zero. The navigator hit "home" on her GPS and the two pilots vectored toward a second airfield in Jordan.

That left the "flyboys."

Two passes and the F-18s fled the scene. Punch for 25,000 feet and hope the sandpaper stayed out of turbines. Dust had ruined more than one engine in these conditions, and hitting the carrier on a single power source in this weather was no means of ensuring your loved one was going to get a kiss at the port upon return from deployment. The Navy top guns were good, but not stupid.

That left the F-15E. A menace for ISIS that seemingly defied darkness, urban concealment, and most weather conditions.

ISIS jihadi quickly learned to look and listen for the "bird"—and then evaporated into anything that seemed like a safe hiding place.

But the damn dust was an equalizer. You could fly above it, but that left the incompetent ISF subject to death and equipment losses. You could fly into it, but that had resulted in the loss of three birds and the six aircrew.

All of which meant you left when things turned red. The F-15s took one more pass in hopes of spotting the remaining ISIS trucks and left.

Too fucking hard to separate friendly from enemy in good conditions, this was plain impossible. The F-15s headed back to Qatar.

ISIS finished the job at Speicher when Trucks Five and Six careened to a halt at the communications center.

This structure had been spared the initial pyrotechnics, and one of the technicians was able to patch a call through to an emergency number handwritten on a Post-It note stuck beside one of the base

SATCOM sets. This was a hotline to a special unit of Marines the Americans had stationed in Jordan, with explicit directions that contact should only be made in case of a national emergency.

Well, this sure as shit counted as one.

A sweating technician could hear the boots of ISIS soldiers pounding up the stairwell as he waited for a connection. He could hear them reloading weapons, hear the bolts slamming fresh rounds into chambers. He silently began to pray.

Then there was a loud click in his ear, followed by an obviously American voice asking in Arabic for the message protocol. The speaker's voice was muddy, like it didn't get used much.

The technician stammered through the call codes as bullets shattered locks on the stairwell door.

"We're under attack!!" he screamed. "It's ISIS!! They're using American trucks to—"

Sounds of a long, dual fusillade of automatic weapons fire came through the phone, and the line went dead.

Back down on the surface, trucks Seven and Eight loaded at a second ammunition depot. Uncle Sam had been generous with the Iraqis—the haul included a dozen Stinger MANPADs and somewhere in the vicinity of 200 Claymore mines.

The Claymore, developed in the wake of Chinese mass attacks during the Korean War, is an ugly toy when in the wrong hands. The lime green "mine" is a plastic-wrapped layer of C-4 explosive nicely arrayed behind a matrix of approximately 700 1/8-inch-diameter steel balls residing in an epoxy resin. The idea is to detonate the Claymore when your enemy is within 50 yards. Think the Boston Marathon bombing accomplished by professionals. The Claymore blast shreds cars, people and vegetation. Great for perimeter security and roadside nasty surprises.

Life on Highway One leading into Baghdad was about to become just that much shorter.

Stingers? Well, there was an AC-130 crew just waiting to die.

ISIS further secured the take, hold, and conquer plan that drove its operations.

Truck Nine was the disaster waiting happen. The ISIS special ops commander—yet another Baathist the Americans had left to rot in the sun—had come up with a means of clearing the "Green Zone." Or so he had told his boss, a moody, would-be Sunni cleric who couldn't preach his way out of an elementary school auditorium.

Dirty, wrapped in reeking rags and "crowned" with a filthy kaffiyeh, he was no mother's choice for the bride, but did understand the terror messaging value of radiation.

His guidance from the outset of the Islamic State's conquest had been very clear: all medical equipment with a radiation sign was to be seized, disassembled, and the most poisonous elements placed within old oil barrels for later "employment."

Truck Nine had 12 such barrels, all full.

And now enough C-4 to spew the radioactive material over a quarter-mile radius, as well as disposing of the four foreign fighters who had agreed to participate in the mission and were now clearly dying of radiation poisoning.

None of the other ISIS fighters would go near the four or their vehicle. Even dogs stayed away, the smell of unenviable demise wafting about the truck like the stench of a dead rat in a sewer.

Time to flee before the dust storm cleared.

Trucks Seven and Eight headed north.

An unholy cooperation between Iranian Revolutionary Guards and the Kurdish *pesh merga* ("those who confront death") was about to be "rained upon" by ISIS. The Americans were going to have to start planning on losing aircraft, and the Iranians could expect to see their Persian empire begin to melt as their apostate Shia fell in front of holy warriors representing the Sunni.

This plan was actually quite audacious. Punch across what had been the Iran-Iraq border, annihilate a Kurdish enclave and then convince Iranian Kurds it was in their best interest to join with the

Islamic State or die defending miserably poor villages in the midst of Shia hell.

Kurds would capitulate and the Turks would pay top dollar for further ensuring there would never be a Kurdistan. At least that was what the emir of the new Islamic State in Iraq and Syria, Abu Bakr al-Baghdadi, told his field commanders as they set out to seize al-Anbar.

So far he had been correct. What the future would bring was up to Allah.

Truck Nine headed east. Through the muddy villages and gutted towns that lined Highway One as it meandered toward Baghdad.

Even in the midst of a dust storm, the ISIS forces took no chances. The lead two Toyota diesel Land Cruisers were separated from the radioactive truck by at least 500 meters. The trail convoy, an odd mix of pickups, old Japanese sedans and a few rusty Russian vans, followed at the same distance and made pains to allow civilians to intermix. Anything to keep the seemingly ever-present U.S. airstrikes at bay.

"This time is different," is all al-Baghdadi—the self-proclaimed caliph—would offer. "This time is different."

The lights of Baghdad glowed in the east ... tomorrow in Jerusalem, tomorrow in Jerusalem. Most Western idiots never learned that the early Muslim faithful demonstrated their faith by praying in the direction of what was now considered a Jewish capitol.

Mecca was a fallback. Another shame to live down.

Chinese bitched about their "Century of Humiliation." The Arab world, or at least the Islamic Arab world, had a thousand years to make amends for. The Iranian revolution in 1979 was a start ... but led by fucking Shia, sheep of the faith.

The true believers were now coming forward.

On to Baghdad.

CHAPTER 1

"Incoming," the lance corporal closest to the glass outer doors softly
muttered, an expression of the obvious. He had just caught hand
signals from the DNI's personal guard, which had spilled out of the
armored Sprinter van in a protective wedge formation. The gesture
meant: Bad Shit Coming Down.

Boots double-tapped the floor as the Marine guard contingent
snapped to attention. The lead guards came through the lobby flashing more DoD gang signs, providing a protective hood around the
DNI. They streamed into the building, past the blast-proof doors and
first checkpoint. The Marine sergeant at the desk had already hit the
button which would alert SECDEF to the imminent approach of his
high-priority guest.

The DNI was a short, pudgy, balding civilian with dandruff and
halitosis. The SECDEF was a potbellied pug with a toupee and den-
tures. Their attendant guards, aides, and gofer-pages squared off like
opposing medieval armies in the DIA briefing room, a vast starry
chamber with a massive platform at its center. Floating six feet above
it was a holographic Geospatial Organizational Display of the world.
Bright dots indicated areas of volatility, while flashing ones indicated
trouble.

A dot in central Iraq identifying Camp Speicher was an engorged, throbbing red.

By way of greeting, the SECDEF bellowed: "What the *FUCK?!*"

The DNI's hands were already up in resigned conciliation. "We only just heard ourselves. We've lost a bunch of assets since the attack, all over Anbar. ISIS is rolling up what's left of our networks. Our read is they're moving on Baghdad, and with Speicher gone, they've pretty much got it already. As it stands right now, we've lost our last vestige of control in Iraq," the DNI panted, exhaling unpleasantly.

Only the hum of the GOD overhead could be heard in the room, quite a feat given the number of agitated bodies therein.

At long last, unable to stand the fumes from his intelligence analogue, the SECDEF broke the silence.

"How could this have happened?"

The DNI's pouched face was grave.

"We don't know."

Truer words were never spoken in America.

ANKARA, TURKEY – 12 HOURS AFTER ATTACK ON CAMP SPEICHER

Muted buzzing of an Avea phone in Adalet Gunay's pants pocket, lying somewhere in the next room, matched the initial sensation in his head as it woke him.

Shit, he'd passed out at Fikriye's apartment again. His own fault, he'd stayed for a bit too much of her hospitality, which included multiple bottles of Tekirdag, and a long, torporous sex session in a cloud of the special opiated hash she got from Afghanistan through some Iranian connection or other.

His head was a wet fog bank, his crotch a dirty, rutted shoulder on a long-neglected road. All told, this was not an unusual way for him to start the day.

He managed to get to his phone while sustaining only minor injuries on a trek into the other room. Despite his condition, he automatically checked to see if the incoming call had tripped the encryption detector on his phone, an aftermarket addition not available on the stock handset sold to the general public. Sure enough, the small red indicator light in the lower-left corner of the screen was glowing ominously. *Kaşar,* he grumbled to himself as he went through the semiconscious shambling ritual of checking messages/fumbling cigarette in mouth/getting pants on. He was going to have to go to work.

Adalet Gunay was a lieutenant in the *Jandarma İstihbarat Teşkilatı* (*JİTEM* for short), the intelligence/counterterrorism ops wing of the *Jandarma Genel Komutanlığı*, the Turkish Gendarmerie. *JİTEM* was, technically, responsible for keeping the peace in sensitive gray areas deemed outside police jurisdiction; this meant whatever the Ministry of the Interior wanted kept out of the public eye. Which included interrogation (torture), state seizure of assets (robbery), detainment of suspicious individuals (for ransom or blackmail), drug interdiction (for resale at a later date), and, of course, murder (ongoing CT operations).

All in a day's work.

Gunay's biggest coup was his access to SWIFT. The second largest bank in Turkey, Ziraat Bankasi, had over 1,500 branch offices and $200 billion in assets. It depended on SWIFT, the Society for Worldwide Interbank Financial Telecommunication, for daily operations and continued profits. SWIFT allowed banks to send and receive transaction information via a secure network that linked 9,000 financial institutions in every country but North Korea. Pyongyang had to send bodies to Beijing for international transactions.

Run by a Pakistani, SWIFT was arguably even better than CIA or NSA at keeping secrets. Protected by 256-bit encryption, the network changed codes once a week, always on a random day. This did not deter Gunay's employees from trying. He might not be reading bank ledgers and tracing each transfer, but on a daily basis his team provided a sophisticated comprehension of overall cash flows and knew when bankers deviated from expected patterns.

In the intelligence community such knowledge was power. In his world there was no trust, no ethics and no morals. Family or friends only served to get you a job. After that you were on your own.

So he'd latched onto the idea of breaking into SWIFT. Screw the *hawalas,* that crazy system whereby you dropped your cash with a butcher in Country "A" and his cousin the baker paid it out in Country "B," he wanted to see everything in writing and done electronically. So did the Islamic State and the Kurds; they were moving way too much cash to trust some bearded middlemen. That, and their weapons suppliers wanted hard currency, not passwords and promises.

In short, everyone turned to SWIFT. Which meant Ankara needed access to the banking system without the delay of trying to decrypt software.

It quickly became apparent that none of the region's combatants or unnamed benefactors were particularly adept at managing finances. Arms merchants were happy to sell to the highest bidder, and there was more than a little American manipulation taking place from the sidelines.

Watching transactions, Gunay became aware of the fact that Lockheed Martin was selling the Kurds drones at the same time a Washington-based entity was turning MANPADs over to the Qataris. Who in turn, not very subtly, passed them along to the Islamic State.

But at this particular moment such mental gymnastics were out of the question.

The best he could do was stick a Murad into his mouth while fumbling through the pile of clothes Fikriye had pulled off him, what, five hours ago? He shot a bleary glance at his watch—shit, *less* than that. He was getting too old for nights like this.

But being a mechanism of the Deep State, operating in a pressure cooker of international ethno-sectarian tensions percolating from a variety of interests that ranged from bodies politic to personae psychopathic, one required a release valve. Gunay's lifestyle afforded him that, but not in ways that pleased his superiors, who had been getting increasingly expressive of their disapproval with him of late.

He found a Zippo in his shorts, atop his service weapon, a Yavuz 16, a domestic copy of the Beretta 92FS manufactured under license to MKEK. A creature of training and habit, he managed to pull up his pants, clip his holster to his belt, fire up a smoke, and hit the auto-redial button on his phone—all relatively simultaneously.

Saeed Refai's familiar grunt came over midway through the first ring. "Trouble."

Gunay shot smoke in broad twin cones out his nostrils as he buttoned his shirt cuffs and snapped on his watch. "Not ours, I hope."

"Everyone's. The general's called an emergency meeting, attendance mandatory for all senior staff."

Saeed was not one to mince words, and rarely brought good news. Gunay sighed and ran a hand through his hair, which was still thick, though now well-salted and peppered. "You should know I'm not in any shape to drive."

He could hear Saeed's laugh, which to most others sounded more like a rhino's warning snort. "I've got the car downstairs."

Now *that* was good to hear. Ordinarily it would be at least a 45-minute drive to headquarters, through all manner of traffic and obstacles. But at this time of night there shouldn't be any, unless …

"How are the Kurd sections tonight?" he asked hopefully.

"You're in luck," Saeed chuckled unpleasantly. "There's police callouts from Bakirköy clear to Pendik. Bigger shit's going on down south, army units have been put on high alert. The Kurds are having big fun tonight. Should buy you some time."

Gunay smiled for the first time since regaining consciousness. Kurdish unrest meant traffic, which understandably meant delays. Which meant Saeed would be able to drive him through one of their prescribed quick routes along the city's backstreets to Gunay's apartment, so he could shower, shave, clean his teeth, change, and down some ibuprofen and B12. Saeed always knew where to grab a quick coffee of antiaircraft caliber, and he could do it any time of the day or night. He'd show up to the meeting looking the part, at least.

They'd make up the time lost on Gunay's pit stop using the department radio and excuse of Kurdish mischief, all of which would paint a taxi driver's nightmare picture of city traffic at that hour.

The other abetting element in this bid for time, his car.

After a quiet divorce, when his wife had taken the kids and almost everything else, Gunay had experienced the understandable urge to own something valuable, that was recognizable as his own, and something which his children might someday enjoy, if his wife ever let them speak to him again.

To the casual observer, Gunay's car was a '59 Mercedes Type 190 Fintail sedan—an elegant, but not terribly overpriced collectible for this part of the world. Prying eyes would appreciatively drink in the aftermarket accouterments—lightweight ceramic armor inside the door panels, ballistic glass throughout the greenhouse, steel bumpers with hidden carbon-block reinforcements, and a KERS-augmented turbo-diesel V12 making 600 horsepower and 30 mpg, to name a few—before Saeed finished closing the snoop's eyes forever.

Saeed had the rear windows rolled down from the driver's seat, another forward-thinking addition. Both seat banks were benches, with unusually thick backing. The rear one contained additional armor, sturdy enough to stop 7.62-millimeter rounds. The driver's bank had an inch-and-a-half slot running down its middle. At the touch of a button, the driver could fire a spring-loaded sheet of inch-thick Lexan up into a receiving groove in the headliner with enough force to sever grasping fingers. A longtime intelligence officer, well-versed in sudden pickups of unwilling passengers, Gunay had designed the feature himself. The thought always made Saeed smile, an unpleasant sight to most.

Saeed wasn't smiling tonight as Gunay climbed wearily into the passenger seat.

"You stink. She must have used you like a lab rat."

"You should show more respect to your elders, *yavru*," Gunay grunted, firing up another cigarette, already scrolling through his phone for *JİTEM* traffic. "You can fill me in over coffee."

Saeed—who ran five miles a day in any weather, often up and down mountains—shook his head, rolled the rear windows up a bit to facilitate his boss's phone calls, and eased the Fintail down into the labyrinth of Istanbul's ancient streets.

CHAPTER 2

CENTRAL BAGHDAD – THREE DAYS AFTER CAMP SPIECHER ATTACK

Truck Nine and an assorted loose collection of escorts made damn good time, all things considered. An aged warehouse near the center of Baghdad appeared less than 72 hours after leaving Speicher.

Iraq's decrepit roads were no small hindrance. Decades of war, punitive air strikes and improvised explosives buried in the middle of traffic lanes left a moonscape even the four-wheel drive Land Cruisers and larger trucks found nearly impassable.

Then there were the innumerable traffic checkpoints.

While they had been waved through "tax stations" set up by villages trying to pay for services the central government no longer provided, the Shia militia "security stations" were a different matter.

But more as a consumption of ammunition and time than a threat to this eerie convoy.

The least experienced member ISIS dispatched on this mission had more than eight months of running and gunning under his belt. The others boasted of years surviving sectarian warfare. Soldiers of the former Irish Republican Army were rank amateurs by comparison.

As such, their approach to Shia road blocks worked as follows. The lead ISIS Toyota Land Cruiser pulled up to a "security station" and its occupants executed pre-agreed-upon targets. Six Shia, six kills. The rest of the vehicles rolled through.

Next stop, the Green Zone.

Located just to the north of the Tigris River U-turn in central Baghdad, the Green Zone had become a safety bubble during the American occupation. Surrounded by blast walls, barbed wire and armed U.S. military personnel, its 10 square kilometers was only slightly less secure than the Baghdad International Airport and adjoining Camp Victory.

What made the Green Zone unique was that it was home to the largest U.S. embassy in the world.

This embassy compound housed over 5,000 Americans. Composed of two diplomatic buildings, six apartment complexes, a power station and water/waste management treatment facility, it was a self-contained village that appeared immune to attack.

But radiation is immune to air defense systems and armed guards.

Truck Nine hit the Green Zone's front gate at 40 miles per hour.

A steel security pole broke off its pedestal, guards scattered like leaves in the wind, and a security vehicle parked just inside as a deterrent to just such a maneuver was left spinning like a top. Random shots bounced off the cab and killed one of the would-be martyrs riding shotgun in the canvas-covered rear bed. But even that nuisance came to a quick end.

There was no security to be found 500 yards after passing through the checkpoint. Truck Nine quickly reached 60 mph with the embassy compound dead ahead.

Even this seeming tactical victory was no guarantee of success. Americans were not stupid or blind. After Benghazi, all vulnerable U.S. diplomatic compounds had armed drones on station and were wired into a sea of communications grids.

Truck Nine's kamikaze run set in motion a frenzy of responses.

Before it made the final turn, U.S. Marines had .50-caliber sniper rifles trained on the truck's cab. An MQ-9 Reaper drone was already assuming an attack attitude that brought its Hellfire missiles to bear, a maneuver highly discouraged but not prohibited in emergency situations.

Good responses, made in good time.

But still too late.

Truck Nine's driver detonated a C-4 "wrapper" 100 yards from the embassy gate. By then his windscreen had been shattered by American rounds and everyone else in the cab was dead. But their mission was already accomplished.

Baghdadi's martyrs vaporized in front of the U.S. defenders. Shrapnel pierced flesh and shattered windows. Thirty American personnel died instantly; another 20 mixed American and Iraqi by-standers died when the drone's missile hit wide of the mark by a scant 10 feet.

INSIDE THE EMBASSY COMPOUND – 30 SECONDS AFTER DETONATION

"What the fuck?!" Best the U.S. ambassador could offer after he'd crawled out from beneath his steel desk.

The Marine E-7 in charge of the embassy guard, a senior NCO with years in the field, wasted few words. "Security breach, suicide bombers, check radiation detectors." A grim warning rummaged from years of warnings by paranoid intelligence briefers.

THE WHITE HOUSE, WASHINGTON DC – 60 SECONDS AFTER EMBASSY DETONATION

Washington knew about the blast almost as soon as those inside the embassy compound. The Defense National Military Command Center was actually alerted before State's watch desk.

Little good that served the president ensconced with billionaire donors in the Oval Office. This was a rude interruption in the midst of a bid for cash. Gucci suits and thick checkbooks still meant the most powerful man on the planet must make time for handshakes, pictures, and be an ear for various pitches, some of which quickly became proposed legislation.

Not anymore. Not after the chief of staff broke in and whispered, "Baghdad just went silent and nuclear."

In response, not even a twitch or loss of the president's famous "plastic smile," only this:

"Gentlemen, we are going to have to adjourn."

The money brood stood, shook hands, thanked "Mr. President," and departed. In less than a minute the Oval Office was cleared and it was a mad dash to the subterranean situation center—a complex installed in the aftermath of 9-11, an underground compound that was over-pressurized, sealed behind blast doors, and connected to the world via a sequence of fiber cables and microwave dishes that linked back to a secure communications center at Bolling AFB, five miles away.

1600 Pennsylvania Avenue never had television reception problems. This situation center would hum even if a tactical nuke hit the Old Executive Office Building on 17th Street, right next door.

The initial feed was grim—collapsed buildings, shattered glass, blood sprayed on streets and walls. The kind of reception that had become sadly typical for American government posts abroad.

"YOU FUCKS TOLD ME THIS COULD NEVER HAPPEN!" The president was clearly nonplussed.

"Mr. President." The first words out of his assistant national security aide. "We thought the Iraqis had security in hand."

"Clearly." His sarcasm needed no interpretation. "Casualties?"

"Unknown." The Defense representative answered the question before his State counterpart could respond.

"What kind of blast?" A presidential query.

"Geiger counters have gone off the scale." Defense again.

"What the *FUCK?!*" shouted POTUS. Not the finest day for presidential transcripts. "I thought we had the MINDS system in place to prevent exactly this problem!" MINDS, the Miniature Integrated Nuclear Detection System, was designed by a group at Princeton University's Plasma Physics Laboratory. It was supposed to detect a dirty bomb before it went off.

"Sir," State finally stepped in. "The ambassador has been breached and we now have over 5,000 U.S. citizens with radiation exposure that is going to kill ... more than a few of my close personal friends." Trust State to go for the humanitarian jugular on round one.

The president leaned back, tossed his glasses on the conference table and took a deep breath.

"Evacuation options?" When among humanitarians, best to sling the same shit.

"None." Defense raining on his parade again.

"Say what?"

"Sir, as of this moment, ISIS owns Baghdad International Airport." Not quite a true statement, but the Defense representative was in his job because, not in spite of, his legal education. He was following strict instructions to bat down a White House penchant for immediately looking to an application of armed might.

"Owns?" POTUS should have known better, but it came out as a question.

"Owns." Defense was blunt. Fuck the politicians, even if it was the president of the United States. Pricks deserved a lesson in humility.

"The Islamic State," the boss continued, "I presume?"

"Yes Sir." State jumping back in.

"Our people *will* come out." Back to a president playing for history.

"Yes, Sir." Goddamn Defense again.

Then silence as they watched the live feed. Civilians lying in the street dying, Marines bleeding out at the gate or crouched in firing postures while soaking up radiation, unseen diplomatic staffers doing the same behind desks, supposed safe walls or in a mortar-proof bunker. A death toll that would never be formally announced.

The president silently wondered how long it would take radiation to sicken all the goddamn TV journalists already on scene, thereby cutting short any video feeds Defense couldn't micromanage.

A very, very bad day in Baghdad, indeed.

CHAPTER 3

ANKARA, TURKEY – THREE DAYS AFTER THE ATTACK AT CAMP SPEICHER

Saeed was a pragmatist. He had learned well from Chinese instructors at his school in Beijing. Raised by a father who once had been Ankara's representative to Jiang Zemin's "royal court," Saeed was offered a unique opportunity to study different ways of thinking and thriving.

His lessons emphasized a simple fact: better to be alive and wealthy than to be famous or tied to an ideology.

His friends hated the resultant aloof attitude; he could sit through Friday prayers and then attend a quiet party, complete with nicely iced Jack Daniel's.

His thought, verbally unexpressed—Israelis drank, Saudis drank, shit, even Iranians drank. Why not him? Helped smooth rough waters during business discussions, and there was always hope an adversarial member of the conversation would make a stupid or even fatal mistake upon consuming too much good scotch.

As a pragmatist, he liked the Berretta 9mm pistol. While others complained about its weight, he found the gun to be dependable and accurate, even at 50 meters.

His other wet work depended on a much-beloved M-4.

Wonderful weapon. Shorter barrel than the M-16. Recoil was so minimal he could sit on the range and shoot with eye-glasses pressed to the scope. Turn on the laser pointer and night was just another good time to operate.

Arguments over where his mission ended and the Turkish military's began, caused quite the heated discussion across Ankara's national security apparatus. And endless bureaucratic pain for Gunay.

That debate ended when another of Saeed's colleagues was killed by ISIS mortar crews. No more arguments now. Ankara was determined to defend its national borders at any cost. Turn the Kurds on each other, let the Syrians kill their own, and facilitate ISIS activities to further stir this angry lot.

A job uniquely suited for his talents and contacts.

The Islamic State wanted him dead, the Palestinians wanted him dead, and the Israelis had his picture on "most wanted" posters. The only thing that kept the Mossad at bay was Ankara's threat to respond in kind.

However, winds of war change.

Doha made it clear to the leadership in Ankara that this killing spree needed to halt. Qatari money had paid for the Islamic State, the Muslim Brotherhood, and a host of lower-profile Sunni movements intended to stem a perceived Saudi monopoly on Middle Eastern politics.

Ankara, however, saw an opportunity to turn this mayhem into an advantage for President Erdogan's own ambitions—a new Ottoman Empire—and ordered Gunay engage with his best assets.

So, Saeed spent much of his time wandering the deserts in search of information and targets, facilitating his president's agenda.

Ankara took significant advantage of Washington's terrorism myopia. Americans could strike from 15,000 feet and not fear the consequences. If a U.S. pilot missed Islamic State thugs, he would likely kill PKK terrorists or other undesirables meandering lawlessly south of Turkey's border. Erdogan's loyalists could not believe their luck.

Saeed was significantly more skeptical about the outcome of such perceived fortuitous happenstance. And so he continually trolled for sources and targets—not yet aware of events in Baghdad.

DOHA, QATAR – THREE DAYS AFTER THE ATTACK
AT CAMP SPEICHER

With a land mass totaling 5 percent of Saudi Arabia and outnumbered 13 to one when it came to a head count comparing the populations of both countries, Qatar seemed a poor contender for Gulf dominance. And yet, that is exactly what the current Emir actively sought to achieve. Employing cash, journalists and even his military, the Qatari royal family courted favor and influence that appalled their conservative neighbors.

In short, Doha was going to put Riyadh back in its place. The Emir didn't have the physical wherewithal for such an act—American administrations had sold the House of Saud too much military equipment over the years and spent a lot of time training the Saudi National Guard. Saudi troops, unlike the Iraqis, actually aimed when pulling a trigger.

This left diplomatic maneuvers and proxies. The diplomats were good. They kept the Saudis from threatening to crush their up-start neighbor.

Proxies were even better.

Al Jazeera spread propaganda that stirred restless populations across the region. The Muslim Brotherhood had created chaos in Cairo. And now the Islamic State was going to be a bedrock of Sunni domination under the Emir's influence instead of Saudi Wahhabi convictions. As far as the Qatari elite were concerned Saudis could return to Bedouin tents, and wiping their asses with the left hand.

Baghdadi and his Islamic State were hardly a preferred option, but members of the Emir's trusted inner circle assured him that this riff-raff would be readily defeated once Baghdad and Damascus were in Qatari-led Sunni hands.

Thus he agreed paying for more jihadi warriors was an option. The Saudi's were not the only ones with an expendable pool of young people. Algeria, Egypt, Jordan, Libya, and Tunisia all had youth to spare. The trick was luring in suitable candidates. Men and women with the appropriate warrior spirit.

As for the opposition. Well, the ISF was a pushover, its men more likely to run than fight, often leaving behind valuable arms, vehicles and uniforms. The Shia militia were little better. Occasional contact with Sadr's riotous lot was typically a waste of AK-47 ammunition. They would simply hold the trigger and spray lead until running out of bullets—a force that didn't bother to aim. Even new ISIS trainees found this a survivable event, with losses at less than 10 percent.

The Syrians were a tougher nut to crack. Assad had managed to reunite the Western half of his country, but only under draconian police-state tactics and with a heavy Russian footprint. Even so, al-Baghdadi kept nibbling away, seizing territory and cities Assad simply could not afford to defend.

To the Emir's delight, ISIS leadership kept track of it all. Running a quasi-government and crafting a durable, efficient defense force required statistics. Islamic State strategists understood that one measures what one cares most about. This data was readily available to their adversaries, but who cared? Each new posting online saw another surge in volunteers.

The Qataris went so far as to hire Web developers and IT gurus who ensured that ISIS social communications and databases were protected from NSA hackers. This relatively paltry expenditure of money and manpower helped draw raw jihadi recruits and engender more squabbling among the loose coalition linking Ankara, Baghdad, Tehran and Washington.

But even this bid for information dominance and controlled chaos was insufficient to meet demands from an ambitious Emir. He wanted results, now. That meant freeing al-Baghdadi from endless air strikes.

The solution to this problem? The Emir went into consultation with his circle of trusted advisors in Qatar's version of the Pentagon's "bubble"—a conference room continually swept for listening devices and entered only with personal invitation from the monarch.

"If you wish to be rid of gnats, you must kill a significant number." Sage advice from his oldest son.

"They will not listen to reason or abandon the effort without pain from their own population." Another wise observation from his eldest offspring.

"Let us find someone who is capable of taking away their technological edge, who can cause loss of airframes without drawing attention to the Emir." An observation proffered by the Qatari defense minister.

"The American way of war is death from above and few soldiers on the ground. Take away this advantage and we open the door to al-Baghdadi and his jihadi swarm."

This comment drew nods from around the room. Teacups were lifted for a long sip and then placed back on porcelain saucers.

"Where do we find such a capability?" The Emir's turn to ask questions. Not that he had to request a turn; this was no democracy.

"I know just the man." The defense minister again. "He comes with a reputation for well-crafted operations and has no friends in the Washington security or intelligence circles."

"How do you know of him?" The Emir was now curious but also cautious. The defense minister knew too damn many Americans as far as the Qatari monarch was concerned.

"Do you recall the battle in the New York City subway a while back?" The defense minister was polite, but obscure American history was not the Emir's strong point.

"Vaguely." A royal response that masked ignorance.

"One man caused it. He is known only by his codename—ODIN. I know ODIN is ex-military, former U.S. Army Special Forces, has extensive combat experience in Iraq, and good working knowledge of the terrain and languages. He is also a master of military technologies, particularly encrypted communications for weapons systems."

The defense minister paused to let this sink in, baiting the hook.

"Rumor is that he is available for the right price."

"He would kill his own countrymen, his fellow soldiers?" This was not as incredulous a query as might be thought; after all, the Emir paid people to do exactly the same thing across the Middle East every day.

"ODIN is a professional. Men of his caliber focus on mission and means, not historic allegiances or nationality. A perfect soldier." At this point the defense minister ceased comment. He knew the Emir well enough to understand a sales pitch was unnecessary. Results were all that counted.

Silence around the room. Cost was not an issue, Qatar had the money for anything—natural gas reserves under their control were a seemingly endless blessing. The collected men silently contemplated this option and waited.

"Find this man ODIN, very quietly." Final verdict from the Emir. The defense minister had his marching orders.

CHAPTER 4

The raspy Marine who took that last call from Camp Speicher and then hacked into the U.S. Embassy security cameras covering the Green Zone, quietly evaluated data and appeared to be planning courses of action—or so supposed the men who worked for and around him.

The base commander, an "ate-up" Naval Academy grad who made 0-4 on his name rather than performance, had long ago learned he was not going to get lengthy assessments from this "aged" NCO. He heard less than 10 words from the man since More reported for duty over three months ago.

The Academy grad settled for administrative duties, leaving More to the hands of his operations counterpart, a big, sullen Arab-American Army major with Special Forces written all over him.

USARSOF Major Kaysan Faheem could offer little further detail on More than his dipshit CO. He had never received a full brief on the man, but what information he lacked from Washington, he got aplenty from his daily observations of the silent MARSOC operator.

Tasked with providing a contingent force in the event his covert QRF ran into trouble, the major had been informed through back-channels from the CJCS himself that he would get the "best and brightest." That amounted to a squad of loudmouth Recon Marines, a surly platoon of Army Rangers, a handful of standoffish Air Force JTACs and More.

Faheem wrote off most of the bunch as trigger-happy goons who spent nearly all of their time at the base gym or firing range. He'd never actually worked with JTACs,—Air Force NCOs who wore Ranger tabs, had combat infantry badges, and spoke pilot like the actual geeks flying USAF planes. They read books and lived in the intelligence vault. Socialized with no one.

Except More, on rare occasions. The one man who appeared to have little use for any form of human contact and none whatsoever for the chain of command. Faheem regularly watched More walk right through clouds of brayed profane orders from senior officers (himself included) without breaking stride.

No "Yes Sir," no salutes, not even eye contact. More completely ignored rank, running on his own rhythm. After a month of this, Faheem decided to disengage, watch and learn.

Observation is an art. His Army SOF instructors at least had that bit of wisdom right on the mark.

More had his own billet in the mobile homes usually reserved for senior officers and VIP civilians (when there were any). Real "luxury," 25-foot trailers divided into two rooms with a shared head and shower between them. Cold in the winter, hot in the summer, these units nonetheless offered privacy, Wi-Fi, and even AC. Paradise, for this posting. The other Marines bunked six to a trailer without running water, and couldn't whack off without an irritated audience.

The one time Faheem confronted More, a chest-puffed complaint about a missed salute, it drew a long-distance reaming from Langley. A phone call from HQ CIA less than 15 minutes after the incident. That was about the time Faheem decided to leave More the fuck alone, a tactic reinforced when he stumbled upon the trip wires around More's billet. No explosives attached, just alarm bells jingling inside the hooch.

Which saved him a second CIA shagging over More's personal motor pool.

The Kuwaitis had thoughtfully ponied up a fleet of diesel Toyota Land Cruisers. These were parceled out grudgingly, rank and priority being the deciding factors. Not so for More, who commandeered one, swapping the stock ignition setup for a custom of his own design, thus preventing anyone else on base from using the vehicle.

He'd also upgraded the cooling system—a visible length of silicone hose snaked around grill posts outside the radiator—as well as covering every square inch of the exterior with gear. A set of four full-size spare tires. Jerricans with distilled water, others for extra fuel. An LVOSS combination smoke/grenade launcher pilfered from one of the base Humvees (somehow accomplished without a peep from the base CO). And—Faheem couldn't believe it—a fucking Kawasaki KLR650 dirt bike hanging on a homemade brace across the tailgate. The damn thing drank diesel just like the truck. Again, nobody on base said shit.

More's pimped-out Land Cruiser was at the gym every morning by 0500. Was at the Command Post—in a reserved spot—by 0730—and returned to the trailer about 2200. No one ever saw him in the chow hall—four trailers welded together with a mortar shield bolted in place atop the mess.

He picked up mail three times a week—large packages that occasionally smelled like Listerine—and left his laundry with the hired contractor for a "separate" wash and pressing twice a week. Even had his own cell phone—an outsized iPhone covered in a box Faheem figured was blast proof—despite strict rules to the contrary.

Fucking More. He appeared to be living a charmed life, but it seemed to Faheem that More was waiting for something, permanently "On Hold."

An illusion utterly destroyed in the minutes following al-Baghdadi's attack on the embassy in Baghdad.

More was standing in front of Faheem's desk less than five minutes after the call came in on a secure command line. Faheem listened in stunned silence, still processing the news, as More gutturally recited a shopping list in his weird gnarled croak.

"Six men, I pick them."

"I select the weapons and load-out."

"We take my vehicle plus three more Land Cruisers."

End of a very one-way conversation. More was already out the door before Faheem could respond.

They still didn't have all the facts, not even the Geiger counter readings. But a switch had been thrown in Faheem's mind, from staying safe in this on-base limbo with assholes like his boss, to riding out with More, wherever the hell he was going.

A decision made in a moment—abetted by the shrieks from the Academy grad's office as other NCOs reported in on More's sudden acquisition of men and supplies. He could stay here in the rear and gather dust or ride with a man who was intent on accomplishing a mission. Faheem opted for mission—let the Navy puke gather chest ribbons by driving a desk chair.

With one hand, Faheem set about putting his desktop computer on secure lockdown. With the other, he opened the upper-right drawer in his desk and pulled out his service sidearm, a well-oiled Beretta 92FS in a tactical thigh holster.

His final stop with the Academy grad went as expected. The Navy 0-4 declared Faheem had no orders and Faheem reminded the Academy grad that he had no balls. Americans were dying and he was not going to sit here and watch. End of conversation. The Academy grad could file UCMJ complaints when the team returned, if they returned.

More's choice of a team revealed a keen eye and surprising bit of psychology. The Marine Recon boys and Army Rangers turned out to be fellow gym rats who, Faheem realized, were reserved actors with remarkable marksmanship.

More's selection of the JTAC was a harder nut to crack. Turns out he'd exposed a handful of the USAF types to his stash of Defiant whiskey. He then must have racked and stacked the JTAC crowd based upon their ability to handle booze and tell a coherent tale about death from above. Specifically, how one managed to vector munitions into villages and diplomatic compounds with minimal collateral damage.

As such, Faheem knew More settled on an NCO with no family, four tours in Afghanistan, and a Masters in Fine Arts from Columbia. A USAF geek who held his own on the firing range and ran a sub-40-minute 10K after an hour of lifting every day of the week.

This gave Faheem a team composed of the JTAC, two Arab-Americans from Detroit who called the Marine Corps home, and three Rangers: one from NYC, the second out of LA, and the third from the hard streets of Chicago. All five had criminal records that included UCMJ violations.

In any case, all team members were over 40 and very conscious of the fact a slip-up in this world was fatal.

No small talk—Faheem headed straight for where he knew More was headed—the armory. In a Land Cruiser "borrowed" from the motor pool NCO's personal stash. No turning back now. Act first, beg permission later.

Holy shit, Faheem thought when he caught up with More, this guy was loading out for Tora Bora.

Two 60mm M225 mortars with 60 rounds. Two .50-caliber sniper rifles and a case of Armor-Piercing (AP), Mk 263 Mod 2. Eight M-4s with night scopes and grenade launchers. One look from More and the supply clerk stopped keeping count of the ordnance going out. A Berretta 9mm for everyone, plus an extra one with two boxes of brass for each truck's glove box (Faheem had counted a third Land Cruiser parked outside the armory, in addition to the one he himself had just stolen and More's personal ride). Then came 10 AK-47s— always better to use weapons you can reload with an adversary's stockpile. Then the big bangs—25 Claymore mines and 4 Stinger

SAMs (More, Faheem mused distantly, must have thought ISIS had suddenly grown an air force).

By now the three Land Cruisers were loaded with enough equipment for a standard infantry platoon. And More still wasn't finished.

"Shotguns."

The supply clerk, well dazed by this point, just blinked.

"Shotguns, asshole."

The E-5 clerk walked back to a secured wall locker and pulled a separate set of keys out of his pocket. The second he popped the lock, More shoved him aside and continued shopping.

Six Stoeger 12-gauge double barrels with a single trigger. Came from the factory with 36.5-inch barrels—a few barks from More to the rest of his personal goon squad ensured these were sawn down to 18 inches. Faheem, impressed, used his watch to check progress … 90 seconds per barrel. More tossed boxes of .00 buckshot cartridges over his shoulder. This part at least required no explanation; anyone who'd done at least one tour of duty in these parts knew all about motorbike hit men. The sawed-offs were the perfect onboard deterrent.

Last on More's list were three M249 SAWs with two boxes of ammunition to load drums mounted on each of the weapons.

Next stop, chow hall.

More cleaned out the rice, canned meat, pre-roasted beef and vegetable selections. The ice disappeared into coolers with bottled water. The roasting chickens, which smelled good even to Faheem, were left behind. The TCNs hired by KKR to run the mess had no concept of quality control; any prepared food would only bring endless diarrhea.

Last stop was the fuel depot, where the entire team pitched in topping off trucks and two dozen jerricans with diesel, courtesy of the House of Saud. With a series of barks, More broke the men up into pairs and assigned them to particular vehicles. Somehow Faheem knew that he'd end up riding shotgun with More.

The truck was in gear and raising dust before Faheem hit his seat and closed the door.

Speeding toward the front gate, Faheem had the foresight to radio ahead so the duty guards could raise the fucking security bar. He figured More would drive right through it (and perhaps through the sentry box where the guards were sitting as well). The bar just barely cleared the windshield and they were outside the perimeter, barreling through an open desert, making for the Iraqi border.

As they sped past the guards, Faheem watched More salute for the first and only time. He did so without turning his head or eyes to the side.

Never looked back.

CHAPTER 5

GREEN ZONE, BAGHDAD – 1 HOUR AFTER DETONATION

Dust, more fucking dust.

The ambassador was already covered in this red crap. Now the building was seeping its own wreckage into workspaces. "Blast proof" windows proved just what one would expect from the lowest contract bidder; all of the glass on at least the first two floors of the ambassador's decorative front was gone.

Screams echoed throughout the building.

Things outside the formerly glass and cement facade were eerily absent this cacophony. Dead Marines were dead, the wounded bit their tongues and accepted a Spartan fate. No sense in yelling if it would draw enemy fire.

Their worry was a waste of time. Even ISIS jihadi knew what had been unleashed in the Green Zone was a slow, agonizing way to die.

How long could they hold out before the radiation exposure proved fatal?

A thought very much on Ambassador Dumpty's mind at the moment.

Wife number three remained parked in Washington, as did their two young children. A real DC trophy, too—five foot two, 110 pounds, abs like steel. Twenty-five years his junior. Ran her own nonprofit law firm doing pro bono work to advance the education of Iraqi girls.

Sorry, girls. School's out, indefinitely, Dumpty mused.

The Marine E-7 was back at his office door.

"Sir," more a barked command than a query, "the RSO needs you right now!"

Shakily, he followed the E-7 a hundred feet along a brightly lit marble corridor. At least the on-site electrical generator system still worked. State's design team had been insistent on self-sufficiency when it came to the power grid. Iraqis could never fix their electrical woes and large swaths of Baghdad went dark every night.

The RSO was all business. A former Detroit deputy police chief who'd been with the DSS over 15 years. He'd actually asked for this posting; the only worse two options were Islamabad and Kabul. Known for operating on minimal sleep and an unquenchable demand for statistical reporting on attack trends—a tactic stolen from the NYPD—he maintained his own set of communications with the Iraq Interior Ministry, as well as a select detail of Marines parked at Baghdad International Airport (BIAP) and outside Malaki's compound in what had once been Camp Victory.

The RSO's radios were now screaming at full volume:

"Taking heavy mortar fire—"

"Gas, Gas GAS—"

"Shit, they're dropping like flies—"

The broadcast voice was heavily muted—those on the other end of the radio chatter were obviously wearing gas masks.

"Chlorine gas," the E-7 grunted. "Classic tactic. Get everyone hunkered down to avoid the mortar shrapnel and then unleash this shit. Hangs close to the ground, and shuts down your lungs. Worked like a charm during World War I."

"Illegal under the Chemical Weapons Convention," replied the ambassador numbly, "not that ISIS seems to care."

Ambassador Dumpty turned bloodshot eyes to the RSO, not having to voice his question.

"We can't just park here and absorb radiation. But our evac plan isn't worth shit—we never figured they could pull off something like this." An honest response from the RSO.

Dumpty looked at the RSO one more time. "Play out our situation from your perspective."

"First, you need transport sufficient to move all the ambassador personnel—that's 5,000 bodies dead or alive. Second, we need to plan on rescuing Malaki at BIAP. The bastard parked himself in a former Saddam palace just outside the airport security perimeter."

"Why? He's a piece of shit." Dumpty was not impressed with this additional twist, to say nothing of his disdain for Maliki and the strongman's ties to the Iran-linked Badr Brigade that now roamed Iraq as hard-corps Shia militiamen.

"We need Malaki to provide us local security support and leverage in the future. He's an asshole, but he's our asshole." Not the most politically correct response, but the RSO was no pol. "Third, plan on little to no rescue support from the outside. With the reports of radiation and ISIS at the gates of BIAP, my bet is voices at the Joint Chiefs of Staff are going to press back on White House efforts to order a charge of the Light Brigade."

Wonderful, Dumpty sarcastically mused, now this bastard is a Lord Tennyson fan.

"Any other way of getting our asses out of this pickle?" Dumpty was now grasping for straws.

"Prayer."

"Thanks asshole." Dumpty's retort. "Get those men out of BIAP and pull back the Maliki support team. Now! Let that bastard save his own skin."

Dumpty stormed back to his own office. He needed to assemble the security team to discuss options.

The RSO grabbed a mic from his comms officer and directed immediate evacuation, providing the mortars were still aimed for suppression and not direct fire.

Assured that seemed to be the case, he ordered the two Marine teams at BIAP to hit their vehicles—all unmarked, up-armored Land Cruisers—and head toward an irradiated Green Zone. From one shit storm right into another, but what choice did he have?

Direct them to stay in place at BIAP and any local security force would shortly be overrun, leaving the small Marine contingent to be slaughtered on film for an Islamic State propaganda YouTube clip. Bad short-term political news for the current administration.

Bring everyone back to BIAP and the VA (Veteran's Affairs) could figure out the effects of radiation exposure sometime after the ambassador and president had departed office and appropriate replacements were in place. The long-term political consequences were someone else's problem.

DOHA, QATAR – 1 HOUR AFTER EMBASSY DETONATION

The head of Qatar's primary intelligence agency stood in the "Bubble," awaiting a request to be seated aside the Emir. This was news that needed to be passed immediately.

Formed in 2004, Qatar State Security (QSS) was a product of merging the General Intelligence Service (*Mukhabarat*) and the Investigation and State Security Service (*Mubahith*). The Emir found it easier to monitor a single collection of spies than a nest of serpents like that encountered in Washington. Sixteen intelligence agencies! What low-grade moron would want to preside over such a swamp of lies and treachery?

Trained by U.S. advisors and frequently subjected to American military senior officer education courses, Doha's armed forces had strongly lobbied for their own intelligence function at the same time the QSS came into being. The uniformed officers were at first given minimal capabilities. Fifteen years later they had significantly remedied that shortfall. QSS might be first to the punch when collecting data, but military intelligence was a close second. Hence the defense minister's haughty confidence as he watched the QSS whisperer at work—he knew as much as the Emir, only 20 minutes before this news reached the Emir.

Twenty minutes before being summoned to the "Bubble," the defense minister was being given a full data dump from his staff. He listened, with a poker face, exhibiting no emotion nor making a sound.

Green Zone explosion, initial communications intercepts suggesting a radioactive event—enough to panic the Americans and drive them off secure networks in a bid to find rapid work-arounds. Followed, not 10 minutes later, by news of BIAP and Malaki's apparent abandonment of his self-imposed palace prison.

Allah be praised, now Doha had Baghdad, Riyadh *and* Tehran in a tight corner. To say nothing of the predicament facing Washington!

The defense minister sat back and sipped his tea. This was indeed a glorious day. Soon his American counterpart would be on the phone begging assistance and the House of Saud would be trapped by a promise to never allow the infidels military basing rights in the home of Mecca and Medina.

As "Custodian of the two holy mosques," the House of Saud had no desire to breed another Osama bin Laden or his al-Qaeda ilk by letting Americans back into the kingdom in a large, visible, presence. An evacuation of the U.S. Embassy to Saudi airfields—over 5,000 unclean and their inevitable media, or, worse, *Al Jazeera*—was an unacceptable political risk for a royal family engrossed in a bitter scramble to determine who would next mount the throne.

The game now was to guess what the U.S. secretary of defense would request in the way of support.

Doha was the most likely candidate.

Landing rights, certainly. Then there was the issue of airlift. Five thousand was a daunting number.

The DO at Langley had already been in touch with his QSS

counterpart. Using Qatar's massive Lockheed C-5 Galaxy was out of the question. The beast required 8,300 feet of runway and always needed spare parts after landing.

Plan B called for local air assets. The best Doha could offer in an environment where communications and logistics compatibility were going to be crucial were two ancient Boeing 747 SPs—seating 400 each, plus four Boeing C-17 Globemasters. Problem was, the C-17 was only configured to hold 134 passengers—unless you crammed more in and sat them on the floor—then the number climbed into the 200-plus range. American commanders, pilots and their enlisted load masters would never allow it—the potential for bad press put them off even more than the crash that would inspire it.

That meant Washington would go begging for assistance elsewhere.

Which left option three—subcontractors.

There were still a significant number of freelance "heavy" cargo pilots flying rickety old Il-76 Candids across the Middle East and Africa, cash up front, no questions asked. These were hard-living, daredevil mercenaries, products of the dying days of the USSR. They flew anything, anywhere, once they were paid.

Flying a big, slow target into the worst LZs on Earth didn't faze them—their anecdotal motto was, "Maybe we get home, maybe we don't." Held together with duct tape, bailing wire, and kicks from the crew, an Il-76 could land in half the distance required for a C-17. Best of all, because every country besides the U.S. seemed to own this airframe, repairs were possible almost anywhere.

Unsavory though it was, option three was Washington's best bet.

Within the QSS machinery, wheels began turning.

ANKARA, TURKEY – 2 HOURS AFTER EMBASSY DETONATION

Gunay sat and listened. The communications intercepts were a fount of disturbing news. Confronted with a crisis in Baghdad, Washington appeared intent on cutting a deal with Doha. This would mean taking pressure off ISIS and potentially freeing the Kurds for more ambitious operations. A distracted Washington was typically quick to forget backroom agreements with Ankara.

Perhaps the answer was to offer Turkish airspace as an evacuation route for the ambassador personnel.

A phone call to Erdogan's security advisor immediately ruled out that option. "A fleet of aircraft dumping radioactive Americans on our territory in the middle of a war on the Kurds? Never."

Gunay knew that would be the answer. The truth was Erdogan loathed American meddling in his campaign to punish would-be coup plotters and wanted no further oversight from Washington concerning treatment of the Kurds. Best keep the White House looking elsewhere.

He also reached out to Saeed for confirmation of the identity of the ambassador attackers. His subordinate's reply added a bizarre twist—there are rumors of a Sunni plan to seize Tehran's nuclear assets.

Gunay let that pass as rumors. Tehran was not so foolish as to leave its limited stockpile of weapons vulnerable to Sunni terrorists.

More disturbing was Saeed's report that the Americans had apparently launched a rescue effort headed to Baghdad.

"On the ground, or above it?"

Saeed could not answer the question.

Gunay hung up. No sense in wasting time on conversations of the obvious.

OVAL OFFICE, WASHINGTON DC – 2 HOURS AFTER EMBASSY DETONATION

Back in Washington, SECDEF was on the hot seat. Yanked across the Potomac by a *"RIGHT FUCKING NOW"* call from the Oval Office, he listlessly squirmed on an overstuffed couch that served as a seat for the "near" important during crisis sessions. His subordinate, the chairman of the Joint Chiefs of Staff, however, was in a high-backed formal chair two seats away from the president. SECDEF felt like he was seated in the corner wearing the dunce cap. Bad vibes.

"Tell me how you plan to get our people out of there before they die of radiation poisoning or wind up starring in another ISIS snuff clip." The on-camera congeniality of the commander-in-chief was now extinct.

SECDEF leaned forward, as if conducting a confidential conversation despite a room packed with the president's national security team.

"Sir," he began, mentally shuffling through the various response plans that had crossed his desk for the past two years, "we have the 1st Battalion 75th Rangers at Hunter Airfield in Georgia ready to deploy within 12 hours, along with 3rd Battalion at Fort Benning nearby."

"Yeah, yeah," prodded POTUS. What he needed to know was how many troops he was about to put in harm's way, and how long it would take them to get State's people out of the ISIS death trap. They all had voting relatives.

"Yes, Sir." Polite additive from the JCS chairman. "About 300 total troops and their equipment—light arms including anti-armor—four C-17s and the Air Force is promising an airbridge. As for timing, we should be airborne within 24 hours."

"Is that within or 'about' 24 hours?" POTUS trying to put the Defense team into high gear.

He wasn't finished.

"And you just plan to land them all at BIAP?" Now the president looked incredulous.

"No, Sir. The Rangers will be para-dropped over target so as to lash up with elements of a QRF we already have on the ground, which itself is being augmented by another Marine QRF inbound from Jordan as we speak."

The chairman was now visibly sweating. He was divulging details he knew the secretary of defense was not read in on, and he was doing so in front of a roomful of political parasites all too willing to leak information in the name of self-advancement. The Jordan-based QRF had been deemed too sensitive and too low-key to spend time telling the pols. Not the first time, and certainly not the last.

In any case, it was too late now. The best he could do was keep the conversation at the 15,000-foot level. Tactical details would remain in the hands of trigger-pullers in Jordan. He hoped his trusted agent there, an ARSOF major named Faheem, could keep his mouth shut.

"The plan is for this joint force to catch ISIS between our men on the west side of BIAP and the remaining local forces who are tasked with defending the terminal and Maliki's compound. We then provide rolling security down Route Irish ..."

Another quizzical look from the president. CJCS was dating himself as a member of Operation Iraqi Freedom, a campaign closed out over a decade ago.

"Er, rolling security for the Baghdad Airport Road and Green Zone," the chairman managed. That came out better than he'd hoped. If only ...

"Immediate shortfalls?" The president asked tersely.

Ah, shit. "Ground transportation from the embassy to the airport and aircraft necessary to conduct a NEO of this size." No such luck.

CJCS actually had no worries about his teams defeating the ragheads, not with the unchallenged air support Washington enjoyed over Iraq. He was much more concerned about the logistics of moving a crowd of this size quickly—a crowd that likely by now glowed in the dark.

POTUS ground his teeth and exhaled through his nose. Turning to the secretary of defense he uttered three simple words. "Make it happen."

Meeting adjourned.

CHAPTER 6

AR-RAQQAH, NORTHEAST SYRIA, CAPITAL – 6 HOURS AFTER EMBASSY DETONATION

The sandstorm that coated Camp Speicher had passed through here two days earlier.

Red dust still coated cars, floors and people as they trudged about the Islamic State's self-proclaimed capital. In the past, women, children, and elderly living among the Caliphate leadership had largely kept the airstrikes away. But after Paris, San Bernardino, Orlando and Metrojet Flight 9268, these civilian "umbrellas" were no longer an effective deterrent. They all died together in wave after wave of "Roman" airstrikes ("Rome" or "Roman" was the Caliphate's means of collectively making reference to the West).

Ar-Raqqah was even dicey when it came to fending off attacks on the ground. Al-Baghdadi knew that better than most men. His head atop a pike would win praise in Amman, Ankara, Beirut, Cairo, Damascus, Jerusalem, London, Madrid, Moscow, Riyadh and Washington. The ground threat was not from tradition armies or advancing armor columns. It was from assassins.

Agents from the CIA, Mossad, MI-6, Jordanian intelligence, Turkish intelligence, and the House of Saud were willing guns for hire. The very kingdom that once pushed money and young men into his hands now wanted him dead.

To no avail.

The internet was now an ISIS abattoir of live-action snuff clips showing the grisly fate that befell apostate hired help. He had hoped this would be a deterrent, and in some capitals it was. But in those closer to his current base, there were always "patriots" willing to sacrifice themselves for a chance at glory. Their zeal almost reminded him of the men who'd flocked to the Caliphate in its early days.

Al-Baghdadi sat in a dusty, dark room on the third floor of a nondescript building which served as the Caliphate's current "palace." Interior walls were whitewashed and devoid of pictures. Floors were grimy linoleum, marked by boot prints, tea drippings, and the hasty sweeping of a cleaning man who spent little effort on this gesture of futility. To make matters worse, the cleaning man would use the same mop for counters and toilet fixtures—common practice with third world nationals, utterly disgusting for Westerners. Really didn't matter. The next crop of visitors would bring in more of the desert and detritus of war.

At the moment Al-Baghdadi required time to think, to digest the news that had just come from Baghdad.

Shortly the storm would be unleashed and he would have to move again.

The successful strike against the Roman Embassy was indeed a remarkable victory, but Al-Baghdadi was also a student of history, and he saw wisdom in Isoroku Yamamoto's words upon learning of the attack on Pearl Harbor: "I fear all we have done is to awaken a sleeping giant and fill him with a terrible resolve." There was a long, rough road ahead.

For him, that road had started at Camp Bucca in February 2004. A sprawling collection of tin buildings and large tents encircled by razor wire and a 12-foot-high chain-link fence just north of the Iraq-Kuwait border; this was a hot box containing some of the most radical Islamic extremists American SOF managed to capture alive.

Over the course of the U.S. occupation of Iraq, Camp Bucca funneled over 100,000 Iraqi males through its "legal system." Those not confronted with overwhelming evidence were set free, but not before receiving a heavy dose of radical fundamentalism from the camp's more permanent inmates—a "brainwashing" campaign al-Baghdadi joined during his 10 months of confinement.

The Americans had become adept at selecting the right targets for Bucca's holding pens. Nine members of the Islamic State's top leadership had spent time within the camp's confines. This included the current leader of foreign fighters who came to join the jihad, its now-deceased military commander, the overall number-two director, and—for five years—himself.

Al-Baghdadi made no special name for himself in Camp Bucca, but the former prison commander would years later woefully observe that he and his men did little more than create a pressure cooker for extremism.

What did they expect?

Take 10,000 men, give them no activity or guidance, and then provide a handful of radical, literate true believers to interpret the *Koran* and lead Friday prayers. A recipe for disaster if you thought democracy was coming to Iraq. A godsend if you were looking to re-claim a sense of pride that once dominated within the Muslim world. The Chinese could bemoan their "century of humiliation;" Muslims had a nearly a millennium to atone for.

The first Crusade, which culminated with the taking of Jerusalem in 1099, undid Muslim conquests from 632–661 and had never truly been undone. Muslim faithful struggled under the yoke of Christians, the Ottomans, and then imperialists from Europe, until finally being carved into pseudo-"nations" at the end of World War I.

Even then the insult was not finished.

Western infidels imposed "royal" families and dictated forms of governance. They spit in the eyes of holy men or purchased their loy-alty through Faustian bargains like the pact that allowed for the rise of the House of Saud.

Oh, there were occasional moments of hope. Pan Arabism

seemingly offered a path to a new caliphate, but lasted a mere 30 years before being ground to dust beneath the feet of military and political leaders who saw their way to power by siding with the United States or Soviet Union. That all-too-human lust for power gave rise to nationalism, which only served to sow divisions among the *ummah*, the collective community of Islamic peoples.

Sun only once again began to shine upon this thousand years of shame with the rise of the Islamic Republic of Iran in 1979. Who would have thought Persian apostates would be first to proclaim an Islamic state?

And yet, there it was. Run by clerics and purportedly intended to honor and obey the Prophet's words. Scared the shit out of the West, humbled Washington, and inspired the demise of that Jew-kissing bastard Anwar Sadat a short two years later. Only to be brutally crushed at the hands of Arabs, nay, fellow Muslims.

The Algerians would not brook this Islamic fervor. Ben Ali made Tunisia a sectarian vacation resort for cheap Europeans. The Libyan Gadhafi murdered his religious opposition. In Egypt, Hosni Mubarak mowed down the Muslim Brotherhood with a vengeance that frightened even Islamic academics at Al Azhar, the most venerable of the Islamic world's universities.

It was not only Arabs in Africa who spat upon true believers. The House of Saud rounded up the most pious in secret prisons, Jordan's Hashemite Kingdom sold out to Washington, and in Iraq, Saddam, like his Baathist counterpart in Damascus, buried the pious with socialism, that doorstep to the abandonment of all religion. Having Saddam astride the Muslim faithful was no less insulting than allowing Salman Rushdie to read from his *Satanic Verses* within a mosque.

And so it remained until 2003, when the Americans—yes, the fucking Americans—set loose a jihad at the very moment it seemed most in danger.

Saddam, predictably, stood no chance in the face of American firepower, but the Romans had not counted on the opposition resident within the Sunni faithful. The dictator and his security apparatus gone, the Sunni could finally begin eliminating a Shia plague.

While al-Baghdadi rotted in prison, Abu Musab al-Zarqawi ran roughshod throughout Iraq, scaring the shit out of the Americans, who thought they could govern a country of over 30 million with 200,000 soldiers who were afraid to leave their fortresses or step outside an armored vehicle.

The man who would die in 2006 at the hands of a cowardly pilot vectoring in a 500-pound munition from 15,000 feet above his intended victim would give birth to the Islamic State. True warriors looked their opponent in the eye, not through cross hairs connected to a computer.

A shame, a shame.

But not a complete loss.

Zarqawi's death weakened the insurrection and abetted further arrests.

Imagine, Saddam's Baathists and Al-Baghdadi's converts locked within the same gates. At first they would neither speak nor pray together. Then it became clear each had something to offer the other. The Baathists brought organizational skills and military discipline. The jihadists brought the one thing the Baathists had been unable to master—a sense of purpose. The future of the Middle East was being determined within the razor wire and dusty tents of a detention compound that could hold men's bodies, but not their ambitions and eternal souls.

That was almost 20 years ago. How the world had changed.

Washington's cowardly abandonment of Baghdad in 2011 over a paperwork dispute set the stage for his return to the jihad. Nearly driven into extinction by the American campaign to kill Zarqawi, what Washington called al-Qaeda in Iraq transformed into the Islamic State of Iraq in late 2006.

The promise of spoils to be won, land to be conquered, and people to educate through practice of Sharia law all proved too tempting.

The bastards in Washington nearly killed the movement with their mercenary "Sons of the Awakening," a program that paid Sunni men to kill other Sunni for a mere $200 a month. Al-Baghdadi fled to the wastelands of Syria, where no one asked questions and security was nearly non-existent.

He would likely still be living as a goat herder had it not been for "Arab Spring." Allah bless the children of Tunisia, Egypt and Syria. Suddenly the autocrats were too busy scrambling for survival to pay attention to his ambitions. Syrian borders parted like the Red Sea for Moses. Ah, yes, he knew the Bible as well as he knew the Koran; that doctorate in Islamic Studies still proved useful. The pseudo-pious politicians in Western capitals were always more malleable when addressed in terms they understood and could repeat to the sheep.

March 2011 opened the door. The Assad regime was under attack and oppressive security in major cities and online was suddenly gone. Two bloody years later, his new domain spanned a third of Syria and half of Iraq. The Islamic State was finally a reality.

What had gone wrong?

What indeed?

As a student he had read Nietzsche's *Genealogy of Morals*. Now, his warriors were not employing increased cruelty to enhance their prestige—they were seeking to make Sharia real, to correct the wayward and to instruct those who might be tempted to stray. It was altruism, not abuse.

Such nuance was lost on the Americans, forever caught up in petty bickering over their domestic politics. True leaders led men into battle; in Washington they rolled out the Authorization for Military Force (AUMF), a legal dodge that had brought hellfire to bin Laden in 2001 and Saddam in 2003, without legally declaring war.

There was a much simpler proposition in his world. By tradition, Islam divides the world into two spheres—the house of Islam (*dar-al-Islam*) and the house of war (*dar-al-barb*). His was the latter; a campaign against the nations and territories under control of non-Muslims who did not submit to Sharia law.

He strove to bring the house of Islam, but encountered walls and opposition at every turn. There was evil in the world, its names and faces were plentiful. Nonetheless, he had an answer.

The Caliphate.

The words still resonated in his ears: "It is time for you to end this abhorrent partisanship, dispersion, and division, for this condition is not from the religion of Allah at all."

And he had not finished there. Harkening back to the Muslim conquest 1,500 years before, he reminded the unruly that, "this *ummah* succeeded in ending two of the largest empires known to history in just 25 years, and then spent the treasures of those empires on jihad in the name of Allah."

History was now about to repeat itself—but, Allah willing—in less than a quarter of a century.

Now there was a new Caliphate and others would come to their assistance. American airstrikes or not.

Oh, they came. Again and again.

Brothers would be killed riding in the open desert, sitting behind heavy weapons, and in the streets of villages populated by the apostate. "Whispering death," was how they referred to the drones equipped with missiles and incendiary munitions.

Al-Baghdadi did not fear death, nor the might of Washington, Riyadh, Ankara or Moscow. The Caliphate could not be defeated by weapons; it could, however, be washed away by the tide of disbelief, a fate even Saladin had been unable to withstand.

Those bastards in Tehran.

Having thrown its youth and money into the fray to save Baghdad years ago, the Iranians devised a more subtle counterattack—denouncing ISIS as un-Islamic.

Silently, he lamented Tehran had the right idea.

The Iranian line of reasoning was simple and appealing to unbelievers. Reaching back to Ahmad ibn Naqib al Misri in the *Reliance of a Traveler* (a manual for Sunni practice of Sharia law), Tehran spread across the internet this *hadith*: "The blood of a Muslim man who testifies that there is no god but Allah and that I am the messenger of Allah is not lawful to shed unless he be one of three: a married adulterer, someone killed in retaliation for killing another, or someone who abandons his religion and the Muslim community."

And that wasn't the only one. Al-Baghdadi could recite them all: "The killing, if a believer, is more heinous in Allah's sight than doing away with all of this world," and, the Prophet said, "a Muslim is the one who avoids harming Muslims with his tongue and hands," and, the Prophet said, "Abusing a Muslim is an evil thing and killing him is disbelief."

In the West this was called cognitive dissonance.

In al-Baghdadi's mind it was the chorus of inner demons.

In spite of that, for a veteran in his mid-50s, al-Baghdadi was in remarkable condition. His hair and beard were now gray, and his face was etched with worry lines, but the pudginess of his mid-30s was gone and all his extremities remained intact. To the West he was an enigma; the faceless leader who could not be killed.

The American Embassy was simply step one. More would follow.

Allah willing.

CHAPTER 7

AR-RAQQAH, NORTHEAST SYRIA – 12 HOURS AFTER EMBASSY DETONATION

All men are not born evil, but some eventually rise to the occasion.

Hassan Aboud, his *nom de guerre*—wise men avoided divulging the identifier so joyfully bestowed by their mother and father lest an enemy wreak havoc on family and friends—sat on a blanket facing a circle of lieutenants. The bedraggled bunch before him—war is neither clean nor well-pressed—was located three blocks away from the Caliphate's current "palace," a separation dictated by fear an airstrike against Al-Baghdadi's offices would kill too many Islamic State leaders at once.

This was no act of paranoia.

Surrounded by enemies on all sides, the Caliphate—specifically, those identified as key members of its inner circle—was a target of global intelligence-gathering operations 24/7. Disposable phones and employment of internet encryption techniques helped mitigate the threat. Shunning group gatherings unless absolutely necessary, and then only in nondescript buildings or isolated vehicles instead of convoys, further minimized the potential for being targeted from air and space.

Then there were the human spies, those who preyed upon the citizens of Ar-Raqqah and battle-weary jihadi with promises of money or escape from the Islamic State's heavy hand in exchange for revealing the location of "certain" personages.

One hundred years ago this would not have been an issue of immediate concern. Long before a foreign spy in those days could pass his or her information back to those who would do the intended target harm, the would-be victim was gone. It simply took too long for data to make its way from reception to execution.

No longer. Within minutes of receiving possible locational data, the spy would transmit same back to a command post that was ever ready to dispatch a drone or piloted airframe.

Inevitably the fallen soldier would be an operations officer or propaganda specialist. These men had too much contact with outside sources by virtue of their tasks. A cruel joke among the mujahidin world was that an Al-Qaeda operations officer was destined to be the next man to die.

Unfortunately, the same was true for the Islamic State.

With one exception: The Islamic State's chief military operations officer.

Hassan Aboud.

The secret of his survival lay in his anonymity; his past was virtually unknown. The other part was his endurance; despite best efforts from the most extensive war and intelligence machinery on the planet, somehow he always escaped. Even though he could not run.

American intelligence assets had gone in search of his background through a process known as human terrain mapping. HTM, as he later learned, meant mapping the boundaries of each tribe, and determining the demographic makeup of every city, village and town within which a jihadi could seek refuge. HTM then layered on data about personalities known to support those opposing the *kuffar*, cataloguing his needs and wants.

The *kuffar* discovered Aboud once was happily married, had children, and considered staying up late drinking tea a good night's entertainment. Yes, he was conservative and religious, but not in a manner that drew attention from Syrian security forces. Only a fool would take such chances when Assad was still fully in control of Syria.

To that end, his beard was trimmed and he stayed at arms distance from the rabble-rousers.

In short, Aboud Hassan prided himself as an average Syrian citizen.

Until the Arab Spring.

Arab Spring, a populist movement that resulted in toppling of dictatorships in Egypt, Libya and Tunisia, inspired Aboud and his fellow Syrians, long-tired of the Assad family's iron-fisted rule over their country.

This disgust with Assad was nowhere more evident than among the Sunni who resided outside Damascus' wealthy merchant classes. Sunni within Damascus could abide with Assad and his Alawite apostates, so long as the relationship continued to make the former wealthy and the latter left them to pursue business interests in a relatively unimpeded manner.

Sunni in the hinterlands were not so patient or understanding, including Aboud Hassan.

For Aboud, radicalization was a slippery slope that began with deliveries of bread and canned food, and then quickly graduated to violence.

Operating from the shadows, moving fluidly from one hamlet to the next, Aboud demonstrated an aptitude for logistics and recruiting. He quickly built a highly efficient guerilla unit of ferocious anti-government provincials, aided by the murderous toll exacted upon Sunni civilians by Alawite government forces.

By 2011, when the American cowards abandoned Iraq, his force was roughly at battalion strength, his men equipped with a mixture of worn but still functional Russian and U.S. military gear, and earning the equivalent of 140 U.S. dollars a month, which no employer in the war-torn region could even hope to match.

His success in fielding improvised roadside bombs and sniper operations drove the Syrian army out of the field and back into outposts or larger garrisons—creating an "ungoverned space." An ungainly phrase, "ungoverned space." It was indeed governed, but not by Assad. Instead, Aboud and local tribal leaders established the rules by which noncombatants conducted their daily lives.

Then Al-Baghdadi arrived.

Money started flowing.

And he nearly died.

In late 2012, while filming a clip for Qatari fund-raisers eager to offset Saudi dominance in the market for pro-Sunni proxy forces, a weapons malfunction stole his lower legs. In an interview with the *New York Times* two months after the accident (Americans were addicted to media coverage, a weakness Aboud learned to exploit most effectively), he was anything but remorseful: "One of our rockets exploded and I lost my legs. Now we have better rockets. Bigger."

His loyalty and tenacity were rewarded. By 2013 he commanded over 1,000 men, 9 tanks, 4 armored personnel carriers and a small fleet of "technicals," Toyota Hilux pickup trucks equipped with Russian-made 14.5mm anti-aircraft guns mounted in the beds.

Al-Baghdadi provided the money, Hassan Aboud put it to work building an ISIS war machine.

It was Aboud's ruthless force of ISIS fighters that had taken Mosul, Ramadi and Tikrit with the speed and violence of early Arab conquests in the seventh century. Carving a bloody swath through the north and west, Aboud's army had taken Kobani, Ar-Raqqah, Homs, the Shaer gas fields, and finally, the ancient wonder of Palmyra.

Aboud was not a tourist. He had personally overseen the destruction of the Temple of Baalshamin and the Temple of Bel, just as the Taliban had dynamited the Buddhas at Bamiyan. Symbols of idolatrous faiths that led people astray from Allah.

Now they stood poised to seize Baghdad itself. Hassan Aboud was leading an element to cut off the apostate Iraqi government from its best escape route—Baghdad International Airport.

It was time to address his field commanders in the only manner possible given "whispering death," spies, and electronic surveillance. An in-person gathering of weary men, dressed in dirty cloths, but proud of their accomplishments.

Aboud always spoke in a slow, self-assured manner. A proven means of calming nervous warriors and reinforcing a perception of unquestionable leadership.

"It is unprecedented in the history of our *Ummah* that all the world came against us in one battle, as is happening today. It is the battle of all the disbelievers against all Muslims. But the alliance of Romans and apostates does not frighten us. Our resolve is iron, our faith eternal."

A none-too-subtle reference to the coming apocalyptic battle between Rome and the Caliphate outside Dabiq. It was not missed by his men.

"We promise you, Allah permitting, that whoever participates in the war against the Islamic State will pay the price dearly."

As would his men, but there was no need to dwell on that. The way of the jihadi is death.

So far the Baghdad strike had worked better than expected. His intel reports suggested the Emerald Zone was no more, BIAP was theirs, and the ISF cowards were dying where they stood.

The only catch was damned American troops on the battlefield. They did not run from a fight, they had better weapons than the ISF and they knew how to use them.

But even Americans are not immune to radiation.

Hence the gathering before him.

Aboud continued:

"Today, with Allah's blessing, we have struck the *kuffar* in a manner they will not soon forget. The Emerald City will no longer glow at night because of bright lights, but because the Romans have been chased from their temple by the very evil they first unleashed on this planet."

Quizzical looks from the assembled audience. Al-Baghdadi's insistence that Sharia demanded an end to music and television had stripped the Caliphate of radios and visual broadcast devices. Computers were scarce and smartphone users were careful to limit searches in the event their device was seized and its memory scanned for abuses. Living with public strictures dating back to the dark ages meant many jihadi had no clue what transpired in the world outside their neighborhood or battle zone.

"We can expect Rome will seek retaliation." Now the warnings began, the preparation for the inevitable casualties of repeated air strikes. Revenge from a distance was the West's way of appeasing angry citizens.

"All vehicles will remain parked, and tarps, trash or wreckage should be spread over equipment. No group will travel in the open with more than four men.

Phones will remain off. Any change in plans will be announced at morning prayers." Many nods of assent to this announcement, every man in the room was aware telephones were a means to rapid death.

Then the surprise.

"Prepare to move two days from now."

That got their attention. Aboud could see the skeptical glances shared among his lieutenants without looking up. These men were veterans of many campaigns—they knew the value of operational planning, as well as the danger of rushing into battle without it.

"In their haste to rescue *kuffar* remaining in Baghdad and secure the airport, fear of radiation poison will speed the Roman's timelines. We must take swift advantage of that fear to move forward to victory over the apostates. First we find the team of 'spotters' we know are operating near Baghdad. We take them out, we blind the American pilots to our movements."

This had the desired effect. His men understood his simple tactical logic. They too employed reconnaissance teams and understood the value of lopping off such a serpent's head.

"To your places of family and security." His final dispatch upon every meeting in Ar-Raqqah.

The room quickly emptied. Aboud sat alone. Shortly he would call for the two men who moved him from place to place. No wheelchair could traverse the broken terrain that had once been a paved modern city. He depended upon the shoulders of jihadi who would die protecting him from an untimely demise.

The Shia and Western apostates would not take the loss of Baghdad lightly. Iran now possessed nuclear weapons, and even the Americans would be hard-pressed to evacuate 5,000 people. The battle for BIAP would be truly Biblical.

Aboud knew Al-Baghdadi understood this. There was no need for further discussion.

He called to his carriers. It was time to prepare for battle.

CHAPTER 8

50 MILES WEST OF BAGHDAD – 18 HOURS AFTER EMBASSY DETONATION

Sleep in the truck or under it?

Depended on who you asked.

Faheem slept beneath the Land Cruiser. In a mummy bag laid atop a waterproof foam pad. One of the Rangers had chosen to stay in his vehicle with windows open a crack and doors locked, willing to risk being a target rather than sleeping among the scorpions that came out to forage at night.

The first night of their dash across al-Anbar Province, a sniper had taken him out. He was zipped into a body bag and buried in a grave carefully mapped on a GPS that sent coordinates back to a database intended to ensure Americans "never left a soldier behind." Corpse recovery sometimes took years.

More's team now numbered seven.

ISIS snipers were getting better, Faheem mused glumly.

The life expectancy of someone like Faheem was 43. Unless you were selected for command and opted to stay within a gated, guarded compound rather than wander through the desert with an odd collection of risk junkies or thinly disguised suicide addicts. Faheem fell into the latter category.

His father had shot himself at 45, following in the footsteps of a grandfather who'd blown his brains out at 42. The common denominator was said to be booze. Faheem took his family history to heart.

Whiskey simply quieted mental demons, it did not still them forever. He drank heavily and locked weapons in a safe that required a breathalyzer test to open. So far so good. Wife long gone, he isolated himself inside an apartment when "home." The dog lived with his widowed mother for months at a time. Faheem was never sure if the dog thought he was its master or just another visitor. Never lost sleep over this matter … it was, after all, just a dog.

Truth be told, it was the Army that saved him from himself. He made it through college on a ROTC scholarship, majoring in sociology. A high school guidance counselor once told him sociology was an easy major that could be applied in "many places." Right on both accounts.

Physical training requirements were never an issue. He played football in high school and stuck with running and weight-training throughout his four-year collegiate career. The ROTC "summer camps" were actually kind of fun, and he quickly emerged as a leader among his peers. An ability to read people and then inflict pain where necessary certainly helped on that front—maybe there was something to that psychobabble professors used in his classes.

Then the Army surprised him. As requested, he went into the infantry branch, excelling at the Infantry Officer Basic Course, drawing his first platoon command in Iraq and then back for the Ranger Course and another deployment—Afghanistan—then back to Iraq, and finally six months at the Special Forces Qualification Course. That spoke for the first 10 years of his career. No early promotions, but a lot of attention from high-ranking officers.

Faheem, word was soon spread, was an officer who finished his mission without unduly risking men or national reputation. High praise. Even earned him a tour in Washington attending the National War College—an almost unheard of opportunity for a junior 0-4.

Also won him attention from the Branch director and an eventual sit-down with the Army chief of staff.

Who made it clear his experience, education, performance and proficiency in Arabic made him the perfect choice as operations officer at an undisclosed position in Jordan. Yes, the Army had saved him, and now it had left him in the desert with a Marine sergeant who was either going to get them both killed or prove a real bane for ISIS.

Time to find out what More planned to do. Langley couldn't save the raspy bastard out here. Faheem turned away from the shallow grave and headed back to More's Land Cruiser. Army training insisted a butting of heads between an officer and senior NCO take place away from subordinates.

More made no comment as Faheem climbed in. He just gunned the engine and headed for a thin strip of asphalt that still ran through the desert of southern Iraq. Even the Land Cruisers would not survive the endless ruts and bouncing on open terrain. Faheem had looked at the map and double-checked on GPS. The planned route met his approval. Not that he had been asked.

A mile down the road his questions began.

"What's your plan?"

No response from More.

"You hear me?" This was as blunt as it gets—an NCO being called to carpet by a ranking officer.

More grunted an affirmative to the hearing part of that question and remained silent.

Faheem knew this act from watching More on base; time for what the Army called an "attention step." He reached over, switched off the ignition and grabbed the steering wheel. More might be a gym rat, but he was at least 50 pounds lighter than Faheem—who now held a Berretta 9mm in his free hand.

"Think you can find your voice now?" Not really a question.

"BIAP, Route Irish, ambassador, in that order." More's response.

That all made sense to Faheem. Ensure escape through BIAP, proceed to Emerald City, and assist with evacuation.

"Got a plan for the radiation problem? I sure as shit see no 'Moon Suits' or respirators in the back. Shit, I don't even see chem gear." Faheem was warming up.

"Won't be there long enough to need it," More croaked.

"You can outrun chem?" Faheem's sarcasm needed no explanation.

"No."

"You tell the other poor bastards about your 'plans'?" Faheem accented the word "plans" to suggest More was playing by ear.

"No, don't need to know until they need to know."

Spoken like someone who had spent time with the intelligence children. "Need to know" and all that crap. Faheem restarted the engine, but did not relinquish his hold on the wheel nor holster his gun.

"Who do you work for?" A demand, not a question.

More appeared to think for just a minute. "USMC ... and CIA."

Neither answer surprised Faheem. Such dual assignments were not unusual in his world. USARSOF had a long history with Langley.

"Did you plan on telling me that?"

There was a long, uncomfortable pause.

"No."

"Let me make this clear—out here, you and I are a team, I got your back, you got mine. We fight for each other, we're straight with each other. No bullshit, no withholding information. Got it?"

More surprised him.

"Yes."

"Then let's go, the others'll think we hit a fuckin' IED." Faheem figured he'd gotten all he was going to get on this round. At least he now had some idea of where they were heading and a hint at timelines. Gun and run. This was going to be a wild ride.

If they survived snipers, Iraqi roads and, oh yes, radiation. Wonderful.

AR-RAQQAH, NORTHEAST SYRIA – 18 HOURS AFTER EMBASSY DETONATION

One hundred miles to the west, al-Baghdadi was stewing through equally glum ruminations. Sniper fire was not the problem, it was the ever-present drones. Eight good men and another operations officer later, he was graveside, offering blessing and final prayers. No GPS marking here. Just a simple prayer shawl and hole in the grit.

The allied retaliation had begun.

CNN, Allah be praised, was covering the embassy blast five minutes after the explosion.

Well, he had another surprise in store for the apostates and Americans this day.

It had taken four months and 10 good men. All dead when sewer methane gas seeped into the hand-dug tunnel beneath Route Irish. No one had planned on encountering Baghdad's sewer system when the project started. Two blows with a pick had spilt the cast iron pipe and unleashed a filth that filled the tunnel before anyone could escape.

Baghdadi had bought into the tunnel idea on day one of discussions concerning the dirty nuke plan with Aboud Hassan. Aboud not only wanted to create chaos in the Green Zone, but to also stir panic in Washington. Bad enough the ambassador occupants were slowly being poisoned to death. Better yet was the prospect rescue was all but impossible.

Which meant shutting down the expressway that led from downtown Baghdad to the airport. Route Irish.

Imagine the video showing a bus split in half. Add in the carnage unleashed by sniper fire from well-placed warriors. This was more than great PR, it was what would actually drive American policy. Either Washington would be done with Iraq and the Islamic State once and for all, or it would have to commit to a third war in the Middle East in less than 30 years. Al-Baghdadi bet no one outside of the extreme right wing of the U.S. Republican Party was willing to go down that path.

So deaths or no deaths, the tunnel digging continued. They learned how to vent lethal gases and avoid ceaseless overhead surveillance. Whole houses were filled with dirt from the tunnel. Word had been passed. Bus one and the lead escorts could cross the line. Everything else would stay within a firing zone that would make 9-11 look positively benign.

And the government of the Shia apostate Maliki would be no more.

Aboud laid out the whole scheme. Americans would be allowed to take the airport, they would be allowed to control the highway into central Baghdad. And then they would all die trying to flee.

With any luck the ambassador would be left to plea on television, but even that was not a necessity. The fleet of smoldering would-be evacuation aircraft and burning buses would be visible for Google and all other commercial overhead imagery collectors. He would even allow *Al Jazeera* to dispatch reporters.

This was the kind of news that toppled dictators who could not purchase popular support.

And, as Aboud explained, it would close off his western flank for enough time for his men to exercise their true intent—a raid on Parchin Military Complex, an Iranian facility used for testing and manufacturing of conventional explosives, but also suspected of conducting implosion testing—the means of detonating nuclear weapons.

Located a mere 15 miles south of central Tehran, Aboud's sources told him it now served as a storage site for Iran's earliest nuclear weapons.

Even less trustful than Pakistani generals, Iran's clerics had stockpiled their weapons of mass destruction just south of the capital. And then placed keys in the hands of men who worked for money, not Allah. Detonation in place was the easiest solution. And the most devastating. Tehran, a city of approximately 10 million apostates, would be gone. As would the Shia threat to al-Baghdadi's caliphate.

Death, the ultimate form of religious purification. Ask the Jews.

CHAPTER 9

DOHA, QATAR – 24 HOURS AFTER EMBASSY DETONATION

Promising the Emir a solution to neutralizing American air power over Iraq and Syria was one thing, delivering on that promise was another. One would think a defense minister with his own intelligence service could answer the mail in 24 hours. Not the case with tracking down ODIN.

As he would eventually discover, the elusive computer wizard had chosen to park on Bali following the events in New York City. His spies indicated there was another player in this game, but could come back with nothing definitive. Appeared ODIN's nemesis was elusive as the man himself.

A real shame. The defense minister had learned it was sometimes easier to locate a target by finding his or her adversary than via a scrub for the person in question. Bali proved a good place to sit out an adversary's wrath. Leave the dive of Kuta Beach and flee Denpasar. Let the taxi meander through Ubud—cultural center of the island. The batik dyes embellished on cotton shirts and pants were inexpensive and cool in the humid depths of Bali's equatorial winter and summer. Flee north. Past the temples, the national parks and estates purchased by rock stars who thought they would find mental nirvana in the peaceful souls who resided on the earth's least obtrusive vacation hideaway. People knew of Bali, they did not know it.

But even island mysteries are not immune to modern surveillance techniques and the employment of cash. Pay enough "civilians" and one almost certainly will provide locational data.

Contact came in the form of a lead from the Russians. Seemed ODIN employed an encryption method that burned hours of time on national systems designed to crack just such coding. Frustrating for the intelligence geeks who worked such issues and naturally reached out to trusted counterparts, even if they were on opposing sides. (The monetary reward for cracking such tough cases was often worth the risk.)

From there it was a matter of following up on leads—naturally to Russia.

As best the defense minister could tell, ODIN had no faith in Norton or Kaspersky.

Qatari intelligence analysts warned him, Norton was just a corporate elephant trampling consumers in an electronic jungle. Kaspersky was headed in another direction. One morning Americans would awake to cleaned out bank accounts and credit cards that no longer functioned. Kaspersky, he was told, was simply waiting for the Kremlin to offer the right protections.

ODIN, his sources warned, could be headed down a similar path—theft on a grand scale, no guns required. Too late for such second guessing now, he had promised the Emir.

More sleuth work, he ordered the Qatari intelligence spooks to find a lure that would bring ODIN into their camp. Time to touch base with the Americans, Brits, French and Israelis. Intelligence sharing is done through backchannels, and often without knowledge of the national executive. He demanded they pull every string, within the hour.

Turned out ODIN appeared to have been unemployed at least a year and might need the work. If for no other reason than to stay in the game.

And so, now ODIN was sitting in a hotel room in Doha that no mere mortal would be willing to afford. Five-star accommodations came easy when you flashed the Emir's credentials and threatened background investigations for every staffer.

The defense minister kept the man called ODIN waiting for less than 60 minutes. In style, a luxury suite 80 floors above the Persian Gulf with floor-to-ceiling windows, a king-size bed, and his choice of bedmates, of varied ethnic flavors. Or so the envelope handed to him in the waiting airport limousine had promised.

Monitored on multiple cameras, it was obvious to the Defense Ministry's psychologists that this was a man not to fret. He was observed helping himself to scotch from the room bar—neatly poured over ice with a splash of bottled water. A man with some class. Nonetheless, the best of Qatar's internal security force was already on high alert. Direct orders from the defense minister. ODIN was to be shadowed at all times by a team in Italian clothes and German cars that allowed them to blend in with the well-off tourists and businessmen.

The call came to ODIN 58 minutes after his arrival. Nothing fancy at first, just a meeting in the lobby with a representative from the Emir. Things would go from there.

"Come unarmed," the caller had specified, "come alone."

Well, as the defense minister subsequently discovered, ODIN almost fully complied. Turns out the man's only constant traveling companions were a pair of three-inch ceramic BenchMade knives housed in plastic handles with no metal rivets, unnoticeable to nearly every electronic security screening platform in use.

The blades slid into a small space between the wheels of a carry-on that drew no attention from airport rent-a-cops, beef brains on VIP escort duty at political functions, and local retards drafted for hotel "security."

The other constant was a laptop. Just as the defense minister had heard, ODIN considered lethal force overrated. What the man could accomplish in under 30 minutes online was the reason he was here.

Knowing this, the defense minister demanded a professional pick-up—a Qatari military limo, aka a supercharged Range Rover. All black, armored, bullet proof glass and a 540 hp engine. Leather was standard. Accompanying security was "low key." Four BMW 5 Series models replete with a phalanx of armed, suited men, all clean shaved with very dark sunglasses. Enough to reassure the most wary of potential employees.

Standing in for the defense minister was his intelligence officer. A man who should be able to answer or deflect almost any question to be fielded over the 20-minute trip. There were none.

Even the defense minister, long familiar with such VIP treatment, figured this should be sufficient to impress an unknown man who was a legend in a little-understood field.

For a first-time visitor, the Emir's "bubble" was a monument to excess and exclusivity. ODIN, the Qatari leadership noted, silently took inventory. There were hand-woven rugs from combat zones in Kashmir. A long table carved in gleaming pine poached from protected forests in the American Northwest. Egg cups in illegal whalebone, handles of companion spoons carved in protected elephant ivory. By the Emir's right hand sat a gleaming goblet of South African platinum crusted with impossibly high-carat gemstones from Zimbabwe, both from mines now infamous for government massacres of disgruntled workers.

The Emir himself glared at ODIN and said nothing.

Unnerving, even for the defense minister, who turned to ODIN with an expectant look: time for the sales pitch.

Bluntly stepping on the prepared pleasantries being recited by one of the Emir's flunkies, ODIN nodded at the defense minister, who barked orders in rapid-fire Arabic to a standby IT element. The glass of the picture windows instantly went opaque, while drapes unfurled and stretched, transforming one entire wall into a floor-to-ceiling OLED screen. More sharp commands brought up CNN in crystal-clear 6K 3000p resolution.

Now ODIN's voice joined the command queue, which deepened the Emir's frown.

"Internet."

"U.S. CENTCOM home." Now their guest was onto multiple syllables.

The Emir just watched, his cadre of advisors shifted nervously. This was not what they had expected. ODIN showed none of the usual deference, the sycophancy of Americans desperate for a big payday in Doha.

There were nervous glances at the defense minister; the Emir glowered at his military chief, who had brought this insulting American dog here. For his part, the QSS intelligence head channeled the animosity coming off his boss toward the IT geeks tasked with filling this screen. With content supplied by the American dog, this man ODIN. Who did an excellent job of ignoring rising tension in the chamber.

After an interminable wait of perhaps 30 seconds, there it was.

Within the U.S. CENTCOM URL in full display: the black flag of the Islamic State.

"WHAT?!" The Emir was so incredulous he actually used English.

"We're inside," ODIN offered in a professorial tone. "We now own their network, as the rest of the world will find out in about two more minutes."

Quiet murmurs among the collection of Qatar's senior officials and very select trusted staff. Experienced with press manipulation, they *did* own *Al Jazeera,* but distorting a U.S. military command public feed into CNN fodder was thought almost impossible.

ODIN silenced them all with his almost professorial explanation. "This is step one in putting an end to the allied coalition."

More images flashed across the giant screen. A beheading, civilians killed in U.S. airstrikes, children crying for their parents, faithful kneeling before Allah in an open desert.

All on the website of U.S. Military Central Command.

Now translated passages from the Koran began scrolling beneath the imagery in Arabic, English and Farsi. They were witnessing the makings of a global media avalanche; news networks all over the world would crash their own websites in their rush to cover an apparent ISIS hack of the American DoD.

The Qataris could only stare, wide-eyed and open-mouthed.

"Step two." ODIN was firmly in control mode. "CNN."

The anchor onscreen was a triumph of engineering—chiseled hair, sculpted jawline, chiaroscuro complexion and collagen lips. But his trembling voice betrayed all-too-human emotions.

"In a breaking development, we have just learned that two U.S. military helicopters have been shot down just north of what had been the Jordanian-Iraqi border." ODIN barked something to the IT geeks and a regional map display appeared next to the trembling talking head on TV. *"No one has claimed official credit—wait, wait just a moment I'm getting something from our staffers at the Pentagon, they're telling me that anonymous sources there are saying they are attributing this to the Islamic State. I repeat—unnamed Pentagon sources are saying that Islamic State has shot down two U.S. military helicopters over Iraq near the Jordanian border. I have to stress that we don't have all the information yet, these are unconfirmed reports, we'll bring you more information as we get it, but for now what we can tell you is that ISIS has attacked the U.S. military and there are likely going to be American casualties—"*

The Emir had had enough. It was time to reassert control. But the moment he opened his mouth to bellow, ODIN interrupted him with a sense of timing that sent the Emir's blood pressure into the danger zone.

"Wait," ODIN grunted. "It gets better."

Breaking network procedure, the Ken doll on CNN was a shambles, holding his earpiece and looking off-camera. Stumbling over the words in his ears and his mouth, he managed:

"We're being told the helicopters were transporting the top U.S. general in Iraq." Another bark from ODIN brought up a picture of a

white-haired man in blue-black uniform with gold stars on his shoulders next to the anchorman, who was now visibly sweating into his makeup. *"—to a meeting with the Iraqi Security Forces leadership, we are being told there are no survivors—"*

"Turn it off." The Emir had overcome his initial shock. The IT team was on the mark. The screen instantly went black.

"Is any of this true?" A question from the QSS director.

ODIN only smiled. "Perception is reality." A puzzling response.

"Answer the question." Direct order from a still unconvinced Emir.

"Reality, if you only can depend upon the CENTCOM internet feed for news." ODIN's response.

"We have our own news sources." The Emir's rejoinder.

"That are now scrambling to get this story on before CNN dominates audience numbers." ODIN, the defense minister realized, was no one-trick pony.

ODIN paused for a few moments to let the Qatari squawking die down. "This is what I can do. The real question is how far you want to go." Less a question than a demand for answers.

The Emir sat back and took survey of his henchmen. Only a few lacked a blank stare. The last five minutes had been a mental rollercoaster they were still processing. He sought the faces of rapid thinkers. The defense minister was on board. His intelligence chief was registering. The petroleum minister was lost, as was the head of his economic council.

"What do you have in mind?"

"That was an opening round. We do the messaging, we preempt military operations, and we control timing and temptations."

"Temptations?" The defense minister finally found his voice.

"Where we want to draw the air strikes so as to cause maximum potential for allied losses and minimal cost to our ground force. Think of it as sacrifices to Allah. The troops don't need to know, they just have to be in the right place. A diversion from more important activities."

ODIN was now in his element. The Emir no longer owned his own palatial conference room.

"Then there's the messaging campaign."

That comment drew nothing but questioning glances. Knowing he was now on the pay-scale at a rate approaching $1,500 an hour, ODIN stepped in to bridge a few gaps.

"You may recall the Americans and Russians allow private firms to run software security operations. Specifically, Mandiant and Kaspersky."

The IT lead interrupted. "Mandiant now belongs to FireEye."

An irritating imposition, but at least a sign someone could verify where ODIN was about to take the conversation.

"These will be unleashed to target intrusion attempts, as will NSA. The goal is to strike and win media coverage *before* they can identify the source of all the problems."

"The objective is to show we control the cyber battlespace. The U.S. should appear to be ill-informed and slow to react— in a word, weak." ODIN paused for a moment to let that sink in. "CENTCOM was just the first target, wait until you see what happens to the National Counterterrorism Center."

That comment drew raised eyebrows from the Emir.

"I don't need problems from the CIA."

ODIN suppressed his smile. Sometimes the allegedly wisest people in a room are not what they appear.

"The NCTC belongs to the director of National Intelligence. It's filled with hacks and contractors who couldn't get hired at CIA. Don't worry about Langley—they'll go into panic mode once their drones stop functioning."

The silence was deafening.

"WHAT?!" The Emir was suddenly the chief inquisitor.

"By that I mean taking away the control broadcast signal.

We can game GPS, the same can be done to the satellite feed that keeps American drones in operation. They lose a half dozen of those, plus a few pilots whose equipment goes haywire, the air campaign will be gone. Baghdad's yours."

"A feat the Americans could not accomplish in a decade of occupation? Impossible." The QSS director was back on his game.

Many heads in the room nodded a silent acceptance of his assertion.

The Emir was again assuming a skeptical pose. Arms crossed, eyes closing, feigning boredom.

"You can do this?"

ODIN remained coldly composed. "Yes, Your Eminence."

"Prove it." The Emir was clearly sick of this shit.

"Put CNN back on." The IT crew was a ping-pong ball, bouncing back and forth between commanders.

The CNN anchor now looked to be eroding, as rivers of sweat carved canyons through strata of makeup. Not an easy news day.

"Central Command is now reporting the loss of two Predator drones and their combat load of four Hellfire missiles over Syria. The drones were reportedly on missions to target Islamic State forces when—"

"You'll love this," ODIN said, smiling horribly at the Emir.

"—getting reports of an apparent drone strike on Istanbul. These images from smartphones and a local television crew working in a local playground appear to show armed U.S. drones over a Turkish elementary school. We need to warn you these images are unedited and extremely—extremely—graphic—"

The Qatari assemblage watched the Turkish footage as the CNN anchor projectile-vomited all over his desk.

"Turn off the feed." ODIN now firmly in command.

"This really happened, or is it just a fanciful production?" The Emir was no fool; easy enough to create reality in this day of computer animation and rapid distribution.

"Ask your intelligence chief to seek independent confirmation. Should be simple enough given your country's digital density."

ODIN stepped back and watched.

The QSS boss departed, and was back in less than five minutes. "It is all true, your eminence."

The Emir did not wince, nor did most of his senior advisors.

"You have proved your point and value." The Emir's blessing to go forward. But a bold marching order was immediately to follow.

"I want the House of Saud to understand where it stands." This was not a request, it was a command.

The defense minister swallowed awkwardly, causing him to choke and cough. He may have over-reached in this promise of a one-stop transition in Sunni leadership.

ODIN simply nodded and looked to the visibly uncomfortable defense minister.

Show time.

CHAPTER 10

JUST SOUTH OF AL HASAKAH, SYRIA – 40 HOURS AFTER EMBASSY DETONATION

Saeed was becoming increasingly convinced that Gunay's lifestyle was taking a toll on his common sense. Less than a week ago he had scooped up the spy master from a mistress's doorstep, and today Gunay had him sitting in Syria.

Damn good way to be killed, either by the Americans or some idiot in the Turkish air force. Oh, his Turkish brothers could fly, they just couldn't aim. Or perhaps it was a lack of decent spotters on the ground. Fucking Americans never shared the secret of how they pulled off these feats.

In any case, he was little more than a target waiting to happen.

It all started 24 hours ago, back when he was parked safely behind Turkey's border with Iraq. Ensconced within a Mercedes AMG G65 cocoon, Saeed could now start to unwrap the latest disaster Gunay had dropped in his lap.

Must be nice to serve at the beck and call of Ankara's elite. The worst one had to fear was being screamed at in meetings or sitting in endless traffic. Once outside the envelope of civilized society and well-trained policemen, the world was much less accommodating. But, he had to admit, the Mercedes helped soothe what would otherwise have been a rough transition.

Originally designed for the wealthy who had no conscience, the

AMG G65 came with a 6.0-liter biturbo V12 generating something in the vicinity of 620 horsepower. Even with a curb weight of three tons—plus or minus the Kevlar armoring and bullet-resistant glass—it still pulled from zero to 60 miles per hour in less than six seconds. The all-wheel drive could handle an 80-degree slope and promised not to roll over on a lateral incline until you passed 60 degrees. Gunay had the perfect city car, Saeed drove the best Germany could throw at inhospitable terrain.

Paint scheme for this beast had been an interesting debate. Germans, being Germans, had argued for a multi-layered silver or white—best to reflect heat. Speaking for his government—who the hell else could afford a $250,000 SUV?—Saeed went for a rusted patina grey. From 10 feet away the vehicle looked like everything else in that forsaken bit of the planet, a rusting relic. It took a discerning eye to realize the patina/rust scheme was sealed behind 10 layers of lacquer.

And so he hid in luxury and wondered at this latest set of orders.

"Proceed to Al Qamishli."

You had to be fucking kidding.

Al Qamishli was capital of the Kurds' next dream of independence—Rojava, "land where the sun sets."

An accurate moniker given Ankara's response to this latest development in the endless Turk-Kurd internecine battle. With no complaint from Europe, Israel, the United States or United Nations, Rojava had become a steady target for Turkish air force pilots. Saeed learned from his military counterparts that Turkish airstrikes against the Islamic State versus those aimed at Al-Baghdadi's caliphate came at a ratio of 3:600. A fancy way of saying that for every three missions Turkey's air force flew against the Islamic State, 600 more dropped weapons on this Kurdish enclave.

He was a sitting duck.

The cause for such fervor? President-for-life Recep Erdogan.

Having sold the West on regional stability provided by revival of the Ottoman Empire, Erdogan was not about to let this motley cast of Kurdish zealots carve out a new nation. One Armenia was enough—there would not be another.

Gunay had warned him this was a mission into quicksand. Stick one foot in such a mess and there was little probability of rescue. Ankara would abide an Iraqi version of Kurdistan, but this latest upstart was a no-go among Erdogan's advisors, particularly when confronted with an aging autocrat still struggling to keep the military at heel before passing his regime to a son worthy of such a task.

"Go accomplish your mission or die in Rojava." That was all the insight Gunay offered.

Son of a bitch, perhaps the latest whore will finally stab him or share a dread disease that ends my misery, Saeed thought. He often silently cursed Gunay, a kind of faux bitterness shared among siblings. In a pinch Gunay was renowned for coming up with answers and solutions.

The Mercedes inched forward under the twitch of his right foot. No sense in burning fuel or drawing attention out here in the flat planes of dust leading to his next adventure.

But why Rojava?

He let the thought stew.

AL HASAKAH, SYRIA – 45 HOURS AFTER EMBASSY DETONATION

So what was this crap about crossing into Rojava?

Saeed took an introspective breath. Back to his schooling in Beijing.

Dynastic ambitions require grounding in national pride, mythology, and common touchstones or they will otherwise wither upon the vine—a lesson Baghdadi, Malaki, the House of Saud, and Emir of Qatar demonstrated on a near daily basis.

Recep Erdogan was equally wise. While his near repeal of Mustafa Kemal Atatürk's push for a secular Turkey had clearly rankled the military elite—Erdogan had once served four months in prison for violating Ankara's penal code intended to prevent the rise of an Islamic state—he realized reaching out to a jingoistic electorate required an appeal to touchstones a common man could recall with pride. And so, Erdogan looked back to the Ottomans.

Saeed sat back in the Mercedes' air-conditioning, a moment for contemplation before rolling down his windows and covering the entire interior in a layer of dust and grime that would hopefully dissuade random scrutiny from teenagers posted to Rojava's "border" crossings.

The Ottoman Empire, a claim to history that many Middle Easterners found as enticing as the West's fascination with the glory that was Rome. Imagine, an empire stretching from Algiers to Baghdad. From Alexandria to Baku. From Athens to Budapest. Just think, by 1650, the Ottoman Empire was knocking on the doors of Venice and Vienna. A sequence of conquests that captured Jerusalem, Mecca and Medina. Purging memories of the Crusaders and reaffirming faith in the caliphate.

Yes, claimant to the real caliphate, not Al-Baghdadi's poor imitation.

All lost in the turn of a short 15 years, less than a century before this very date.

It was no wonder Erdogan was racing to adhere his legacy to the achievements of Turkey's ancient rulers. There was much to be proud of in that millennium of empire—and even more to be achieved if he could finally convince a skeptical constituency that democracy was an overplayed triumph.

For this he needed relics—the touch stones.

Thus Saeed's mission into Rojava.

Suleiman Shah.

Took him four hours on the internet to unweave this mystery.

Gunay had mentioned Suleiman Shah in passing. Likely because

the spymaster had no damn idea of whom he was referencing—
Gunay's memory of formal schooling had long been erased by good
scotch and the occasional hashish adventure, but he still could comprehend Erdogan's theme—lash the past to a common future.

Suleiman Shah, as it turned out, was a tribal leader in the
13th century Levant who just happened to be the grandfather of
Osman I—founding father of the Ottoman Empire. Given this pedigree, Suleiman's bones were just as cherished as the talismans said to
be splinters from Christ's crucifixion cross, or the bones of a long-de-
parted saint. Catholics were willing to kill for such relics. Turks were
no better.

All of which begged the question: Where does a search for legacy
end and a suicide adventure begin?

For Saeed this was no minor debate. As fate would have it,
Suleiman Shah had drowned in the Euphrates back in A.D. 1235
and was promptly buried in what used to be called Syria. A previous bid to capitalize upon common myths and touchstones caused
an Ottoman Sultan to have a tomb constructed upon the supposed
burial site 600 years later ... a tomb site protected by a clause in a
post-World War I treaty that decreed:

> *The tomb of Suleiman Shah, the grandfather of Sultan
> Osman, founder of the Ottoman dynasty, situated at
> Jaber-Kalesi shall remain, with its appurtenances, the
> property of Turkey, who may appoint guardians for it
> and may hoist a Turkish flag there.*

Typical Western legal parlance derived from concepts enshrined
in the Treaty of Westphalia. In other words, a state's rights trumped
other ideological or religious precepts. Suleiman was Turkey's birth-
right and was to be treated as same—an aberration that functioned
until the Assad clan proved incapable of governing Syria. Then all bets
were off.

In retrospect, Al-Baghdadi would like to have been able to claim he prevented the Kurds from defiling Suleiman's tomb. Proof of such foresight might have helped keep the Turkish border between the Caliphate and Turkey even more porous.

But Shia apostates beat him to the punch.

6 MILES NORTH OF AL QAMISHLI, ROJAVA – 6 HOURS AFTER EMBASSY DETONATION

This would be the second time Ankara sought to save Suleiman from the Shia. Round one took place in February 2015—a convoluted campaign complicated by the fact the relics had been moved in 1973, when construction of a dam had threatened to flood everything deemed Turkish ancestral rights. Supposedly the bones had been moved 50 miles north in a bid to escape rising waters—but no one really kept accurate maps … close was good enough for Middle Eastern antiquities, horseshoes and nuclear weapons.

Well aware that Bashar Assad was about to lose control of his northern border, the Turks dispatched a brigade into Syria as a means of saving its small garrison permanently entrenched around Suleiman's tomb and to move his remains.

All went as planned, until an unidentified force attacked the Turkish incursion—a subsequent firefight and rapid retreat north seems to have resulted in one large shortfall: Suleiman's bones were not to be found.

Oh shit, indeed.

Until 12 hours ago, when Gunay claimed an unnamed source had dropped a diamond in his sack of coal.

A thin, darkly tanned Shia fleeing on his 100 cc motorbike.

Running from the Sunni, running from the Islamic State, running for his life absent all that had made him—a wife, children, home and quiet business that paid the bills. All this left in the dust with only one guarantee of reaching safety—a small leather satchel containing a carefully swathed set of bundled skeletal remnants. The remains of Suleiman Shah, or so he had been told by a man he had never seen before and would never see again.

"Bring them to Ankara and you are free to live away from this great waste."

Needless to say, he was less than convinced.

No, every bit a struggling entrepreneur—purveyor of cigarettes, soft drinks and cheap snacks would be more accurate. The apostate only finally decided to flee when Al-Baghdadi's jihadi took the money men.

For weeks there'd been rumors Islamic State warriors would steal a march on Baghdad. Everyone knew it was coming, but no one knew just how fast they could move.

Burdened with armor, artillery and Humvees stolen from the ISF, they'd be crossing open desert, ripe targets for American pilots. Everyone knew there was no coalition of the willing, except in Western press statements, but there was no way Washington would let Baghdad be taken. Never mind the bloodbath that would follow— the Americans would *look* bad, and they hated that more than any amount of carnage.

But apparently, nobody planned on a strike that would darken the Emerald City.

The end was near, particularly for Shia living west of the Tigris.

Employing fast scouts, the jihadi were but six hours behind Truck Nine.

They traveled on camouflaged technicals and motorbikes, moving night and day, separately, not clotting up to make easy pickings in some pilot's bombsight.

How they coordinated was anybody's guess, but there was no denying the ruthless efficiency of their plan. First, lead elements had reached Mahmudiyah in the middle of the night, taking out the police headquarters, local radio station, and emptying the jails. Once the armor rolled into town, the scouts took off again, leaving a small group to man a highway checkpoint.

The rest of the pack split up and disappeared into the night.

Just before dawn, as he quietly gathered a few items and secured the cursed satchel, the apostate read a tweet indicating Islamic State warriors were fanning out across Suwaib.

By dawn they'd taken Abu Ghraib. Americans might have closed the prison years before, but the government had simply reopened it once the last U.S. troops left. There were hundreds of Sunni men locked up there.

In the West such men would be characterized as possessed of a blood lust, here it was simply known as revenge—revenge that might originate from a wrong committed two generations in the past or a slight incurred last night.

It did not take military training to recognize the Islamic State plan, nor the ferocious functionality of it. A Sunni-led jihadi blitz-krieg would bring out not just useless government troops, but also the much more effective Shi'ite militias. Everyone from the old JAM units to the Badr Brigades and all their "special group" splinters would grab guns and come running.

The apostate was counting on this response. While his Shia breth-ren threw everything they had at the airport, he would be able to flee his safe hovel, access a northern belt around the city, cross over the top end of the capital, and begin a long trip along ruined roadways paralleling the Tigris.

It was stopping at a filling station along the Tigris just above Maghreb that saved his life.

He went through the motions of buying gas, tea and chocolate, but which masked his real objective of using the station's Wi-Fi to get a lay of the land ahead. Once he crossed the river and headed into Sunni-controlled districts, there would be no turning back.

As he struggled with the act of courage required for this next step in his hasty plan, the amateur video he caught on the telephone screen put all doubt to rest.

Shaky footage—likely from a teenager bearing an AK-47 amidst the murders—revealed a line of men marching up to what looked like a construction site, or maybe just some girders from a collapsed building. Omar recognized a few of the men—all *hawala* brokers—a mix of both Shia and Sunni.

What?

He received his answer soon enough. A tall jihadi struck a pose for the camera and raised a megaphone to his mouth. The rant was customary, about how these prisoners had transgressed against Allah and Sharia law; that swift justice was to be meted out as was written, for all to see. Then the wires came out, a loop thrown over the head of each terrified money man, several of whom were weeping openly and wetting themselves, crying out for mercy.

A horrific realization crashed through his mind when he saw each individual wire was attached to a long, thick metal hawser. This in turn was connected to a winch on the front of an American-made MRAP.

The camera panned to one of the jihadi yelling through a megaphone—apparently instructing a driver, as the sound of a weary diesel and winch motor soon blotted out chants from the gathered crowd.

And with that, the girder collection, in fact just three beams bolted together in a long upside-down U, swung up.

And dragged the money men up off the ground with it, kicking and screaming as the wires bit into the flesh of their necks, blood already visible, even in the bad video. Eventually, the apostate knew, the wire would decapitate each victim and the heads and bodies would come crashing down separately, leaving the makeshift industrial gallows ready for re-use. There was no doubt the jihadi would be busy all day.

The Caliphate was going to take everything.

The apostate had no choice—He would have to take the package north—even if that meant skirting Mosul and crossing through Rojava. Leaving him roadside 14 hours later, out of gas, short of money and still clutching the satchel. Time for another phone call to assure his would-be Turkish rescurers.

Ahead stood what appeared to be remnants of a gas station or perhaps an auto garage. Perhaps they would have fuel.

An easy place to mark on a map using GPS data retrived from his phone.

Now he was on a a collision course with Saeed.

Or so the latter hoped.

CHAPTER 11

"This is going to be more fun than shooting stray dogs in the days after Desert Storm."

Most of the Rangers on board the C-17 were still wearing diapers during the first Gulf War in 1991; they had no idea what the sergeant major was mumbling about. They knew nothing of the carnage felt on a battlefield after 100 hours of massed airstrikes aimed at Iraqis dug in along the Kuwait border or the "Highway of Death."

They were not aware of the packs of wild dogs who feasted on the carcasses of a defeated army.

They had never seen a body where the face had been sanded off as a result of an airstrike by a four-ship of B-52s.

And they certainly were not briefed on the fact that their predecessors had been unleashed in the desert to snipe dogs in order to hold down the canine population and hone targeting skills.

All they knew were the mountains of Afghanistan and ugly streets of urban Iraq. Most were not anxious to return. And yet this 55-year-old senior NCO was busy smirking about how it was "about time" they came to teach the Islamic State manners or that "Hajji" needed to be schooled in behaving like civilized human beings. Mutterings of the insane, sleep-deprived or—worse yet—undiagnosed PTSD.

The officers just ignored him. The junior troops had no such luxury. After 14 hours on a plane that never landed—thanks to an USAF "air bridge" of flying gas stations—they had field-stripped weapons four times, been ordered to sort rucksacks twice, and fed the fucking "Meals Ready to Eat" on eight-hour rotations.

They were ready to get off this bird and do some killing.

That was the plan, anyway.

Before someone decided the sergeant major was going to have a fatal parachute accident on egress.

Not hard to do. Simply unclip from the static line, jump early and then pull your chute after collapsing the insane man's main canvas. Risky maneuver, particularly when jumping at 1,000 feet, but worth every second of terrified screams from a demented NCO—forgetting his reserve in panic--knowing he was about to hit terra firma at lethal speed. No one ever said being a Ranger was like joining the Boy Scouts. They liked killing, and occasionally practiced on a perceived weak link in the team.

The sergeant major was starting to sound like he qualified.

Plus they were just sick of his spit and polish gung-ho shit. Got so bad a small group cut straws from the juice boxes that came with the MREs and then drew to see who got the privilege.

A 20-year-old from Alabama—went by "Pickup," his favorite mode of transportation. Remained to be seen if the cracker had it in him. A betting pool swiftly formed, with the smart money on "yes."

The other C-17s were no better. The current crop would never have survived the weeks on board the ships that delivered their great-grandfathers across oceans to battlefields half a world away. Hell, crossing the English Channel by landing craft would be an exercise in time management and on-board entertainment for this generation. Half of them were plugged into headsets that accessed phones laced with music. The other half were on iPads engaged in the latest downloaded movie.

Nowadays it was so bad the Air Force broke down and upgraded cargo planes with satellite access (reception only, no transmit capability). Better to have electronically mollified troops than bitchy kids with knives and a lot of ammunition.

Bank turn into Syrian airspace. Goddamn Turks were still not permitting overflight. Rumors were out that the Islamic State wackos now had access to new Russian MANPADs. Going to make approach into the left side of Baghdad a lot of fun for the kids in back. Aircrew loved making the grunts sick.

Pilots dropped to a thousand feet, then five hundred, now it was three hundred. The ride was a four-wheel-drive adventure in the highlands of Colorado. No one walking about in the back. Night-vision googles the rule up front. Last thing you wanted to do was auger into some uncharted man-made obstacle. The world's greatest video game at 150 knots. Too bad the troopers had to miss the show. They would get their turn when the cargo door opened and the back end became a dive platform.

The first "thump" came 50 miles outside the drop zone. No warning from the F-35 fighter cap orbiting 100 miles behind the C-17s, and no heads-up from AWACS ("Airborne Without a Clue" was the comment from communications and signals specialists sitting aboard a RC-135 Rivet Joint, also on station). Not that the RJ boys and girls should brag, they too missed the incoming Iranian planes.

F-4 Phantoms. Ancient relics that no one could believe Tehran had the resources to keep flying.

Except the bastards in New Delhi, who found the Iranian Air Force a comforting Western threat to a Pakistani fleet of Chinese J-10s. The J-10 was a blatant copy of the Israeli Lavi and had been sold to Islamabad almost as soon as the first test models cleared factory floor. Great bird for the Pakistani pilots who were no match for their Indian counterparts.

New Delhi countered by providing Tehran with access to spare parts necessary for keeping the F-4, and equally old F-14s, airborne.

American intelligence analysts had dismissed this collection of antiques as "irrelevant artifacts," until they started showing up over Iraq on strike missions against the Islamic State. Then there was hell to pay at the Pentagon and State Department.

The DNI found himself in front a special session of the House Permanent Select Committee on Intelligence explaining why the Defense Intelligence Agency had so badly missed the call on Iranian airstrike capabilities. Needless to say, his answers were cryptic and quickly forgotten. But the Iranians kept on flying into airspace the Americans had presumed safe territory. Things got really ugly when the Iranians shot down a pair of Turkish F-16 Fighting Falcons.

At the moment, all that political hullabaloo was just newspaper headlines for the C-17 crews. Two close passes at this altitude left the cargo planes yanking and banking like the fighter jets they were built to intimidate. It also called for a climb to 1,500 feet and unpleasant demands for the fighter jocks to get off their asses and provide cover.

The first F-4 went down 95 seconds later. "Fire and Forget" was not just a saying for the USAF F-35 community. It meant you located one target, fired a missile, and before the first bird was down you had locked in on a second airframe. Multiple kills were the name of the game. If you could discern foe from friendly.

And just as quickly the Washington-Tehran backchannel kicked into high gear.

Fucking unholy alliance if there ever was one. Rivet Joint managed to establish contact with the remaining two Iranian F-4s at the same time an onboard mission commander connected with the Pentagon. The J-3 operations officer was on a hotline with his unofficial liaison in Tehran in less than 30 seconds.

"Break contact or we take down the rest of your birds."

The Iranian response was concise and on mark. "Roger."

End of conversation.

Rivet Joint collected all subsequent communications and passed them flash-precedence back to Washington. "Iranian birds headed home."

Too late for the Rangers. Drop zone was now at least 1,200 feet below them. Long time to be hanging in a chute when the enemy knew you were coming. The bet on the sergeant major's demise was hastily renegotiated. Everyone was off the static line and on immediate egress. Safeties off on all weapons, mortar teams cleared to fire immediately upon touchdown.

The "reception party" was in way over its head, but untrained Islamic State volunteers at BIAP were still willing to play. The self-proclaimed on site "commander" declared they should be prepared for a rain of death and then began firing into the sky. No tracer rounds in these AK-47s, so it was completely "spray and pray" from positions located some 1,500 meters outside the Rangers' designated drop zone.

Rivet Joint leveled the playing field—time for CAS. What came next was a surprise to the Rangers and C-17 drivers. The napalm strike cost Baghdadi's team of holy warriors 70 percent of the unit. And lit up the landing zone with a bizarre collection of colors amid a random array of silhouettes that used to be vehicles or bodies.

It was the shrieking of men burning slowly to death that no one from the Ranger drop teams would ever forget.

2 MILES WEST OF BAGHDAD – 36.15 HOURS AFTER EMBASSY DETONATION

Faheem watched the mayhem through a set of FLIR night-vision goggles while crouched next to More's Land Cruiser. More and his JTAC were topside, vectoring F-35s onto ISIS positions. Faheem could not suppress a cringe as he watched the six-plume row of fireballs illuminate countless human torches.

"Rock and roll." More's rasp caught his attention. Time to get back on the road. They'd stopped exactly four minutes earlier, when More took a 911 call on a secure line from Rivet Joint for a "danger close" strike to protect the hapless Rangers.

The ISIS defenders were now smoldering husks. More, Faheem

conceded grimly, really knew his shit. He clambered back into the truck, now at the wheel while More worked radio magic. The four-truck convoy up was to 50 mph in less than a minute. Sixty seconds after that, More spoke again, by radio to the other trucks in convoy, no mud in his voice this time.

"Weapons hold until we have positive target ID."

A command that really didn't need to be issued. None of the advance team wanted responsibility for killing a Ranger. They were less sure if the opposite was true when it came to the men floating down from the sky. That lot was in self-protect mode. A collection of beat-up Toyotas was more likely to draw well-aimed M-4 fire than be welcomed as part of the cavalry. Faheem knew that, More knew that ... some of the younger QRF recruits were not as astute.

Rangers hit the ground less than two minutes after egress—and across half a mile of BIAP. The pilot of the third C-17, panicked by thickening ground fire, had gone into a steep climb just as the troops were detaching from static lines. In less than 10 seconds, the entire cargo hold—men and materiel—were thrown full force to the deck. The strength of the Ranger force was cut by a third less than one minute into the battle.

Only their training prevented the survivors from full-scale panic. They formed a defense ring and began firing at any muzzle flashes coming from the west.

BIAP – 39 HOURS AFTER EMBASSY DETONATION

In modern warfare darkness favors the offense. Unless you are dug in and have laid mines. Neither was the case for Baghdadi's warriors. Oh, they had thought to lower the 35mm air defense guns to a murderous horizontal trajectory. They simply did not factor in the brutal efficiency of a Ranger assault on known firing positions. Mortar teams scored the first kills. Snipers claimed the remainder. The west side of Baghdad International Airport was now firmly under U.S. control.

The east side was a much sorrier story. Shia militia units were intent on securing Malaki and his entourage. But they lacked the discipline, skills, and training characteristics of American units. Standard procedure was to stand behind a vehicle or wall and simply push the AK-47 barrel into a position where it might hit something when the trigger was pulled. Fratricide was a given in these conditions. As were vehicle fires, a mass of shattered glass and unplanned consequences.

The only thing that saved this lot was tenacity, stupidity and blind luck. The tenacity came from being 17–23 years old. Death simply didn't register in the brain box. Stupidity came in the form of Islamic State forces blindly fleeing a certain death exhibited in the napalm strike and the realization that whatever the Americans had unleashed it was not user-friendly. The blind luck? Saddam's decision to surround his old palaces with man-made lakes.

The holy warriors were walked into death by machine gun fire, a fear of fire, and the unsuspected consequence of drowning.

More reached Malaki's compound with Faheem and a dozen Rangers a mere 45 minutes after the airdrop.

What had been Victory Palace was ablaze. An armored convoy of highly-polished black Chevy Suburbans Malaki used to traverse the city was largely destroyed. The Praetorian Guard charged with ensuring his survival were little more than a collection of wounded bodies. And yet, within a grand entrance that towered behind a phalanx of sandbags and crew-served .50 cals, stood the former prime minister. As blustery and dictatorial as ever.

More passed on English, his rasp went right to Arabic. "Into the fucking trucks."

Next to him, the biggest Arab most of them had ever seen snarled, "Now!"

Malaki was not used to this approach from soldiers, uniformed or not. Stiffening his spine to reach all of 5 feet 6 inches he stood his ground and barked back, "Fuck you." Little bastard still spoke fluent English.

By way of reply, More shot the security man to Maliki's left, right through the eye; Faheem shot the one to Maliki's right, same spot.

End of conversation.

More glanced at Faheem and circled one gloved index finger in the air. Faheem took the cue, barking in English and Arabic, getting the Shia officials to identify which of the Iraqi vehicles still worked, and the Rangers to corral Malaki's entourage into same. Faheem screamed himself hoarse in two languages, but in less than five minutes, More's Land Cruiser flotilla was bolstered by half a dozen of Malaki's Suburbans.

Faheem again took the wheel of More's Land Cruiser, hoping the Rangers driving Suburbans would follow him closely. At least he'd driven the route from BIAP to the Green Zone on several occasions; he doubted any of the Rangers had done so.

More rasped into Faheem's earpiece on their secure channel: "We need buses, a lot of them, right now."

"Copy." Faheem turned his head an inch to the right and relayed More's "request" to Malaki, in rapid and profane Arabic. Malaki swallowed, looked stupid, and then fished his cell phone out of a rumpled suit-jacket pocket. "So much for secure comms," Faheem grumbled to himself, wondering if the Suburbans had armor.

Two realizations dawned on Faheem as they barreled toward the embassy compound, explosions and lines of tracer tearing through the night sky around them.

Number One: No one in the QRF or Ranger team knew what they were about to do. Remnants of an attack on a U.S. embassy, breached security, Americans in danger—but still no mention of radiation from More or the Ranger Lieutenant Colonel, who should have been briefed on the situation during the cross-Atlantic flight.

Nobody had anti-radiation gear, meds, nothing. Maybe More really thought they could pull a fast snatch-and-grab. Hell, he'd had a damn good run since they'd first left Jordan. The Rangers and Shia would have all died together if it hadn't been for More and his JTAC. As for the radiation, shit, maybe More thought he was immune.

Number Two: If More's primary objective was to rescue the American embassy staff, why had he rescued Malaki's group first? It couldn't have been for the Baghdad bus fleet, which Faheem could hear Malaki was hastily rounding up on his phone—More couldn't have planned that ahead of time, he couldn't have known.

So why had More put the remnants of Iraq's soon-to-be extinct Shia government ahead of 5,000 U.S. embassy staff who were exposed to radiation and surrounded by ISIS units that were rapidly closing in?

What the fuck was More thinking?

CHAPTER 12

BAGHDAD, IRAQ – 42 HOURS AFTER EMBASSY DETONATION

Emergency destruct procedures: pull out the checklists and eliminate anything that might be useful for an adversary or divulge critical information. This left the ambassador staff in disarray. More accurately, it left the State Department employees in disarray.

More specifically, a paper mountain confronting the remaining USAID employees at Emerald City.

The United States Agency for International Development: a bureaucracy charged with putting Washington's best humanitarian face forward. An office that, unfortunately, kept records on every payment made to contractors, foreign or domestic. Underfunded, poorly staffed and constantly under Congressional investigation, the USAID crew held onto every receipt in hopes of avoiding fines or jail time. The innumerable boxes of records littering embassy offices that would allow the Islamic State to identify thousands of so-called collaborators and cut a vicious swath of executions across the Iraqi populace.

Given the fact USAID worked in cash—Iraqi banking and credit systems were never dependable—the mountain of paper would take three days to shred.

Ambassador Dumpty's team now had less than 12 hours.

Fire was the best option.

One immediately denied by security and a declaration from the RSO prohibiting outside activity. No explanation offered. You just were not permitted to leave the buildings. The RSO was paranoid, but not stupid. Tell the inmates they were condemned to radiation poisoning and panic would ensue. Tell them there was a sniper threat in the wake of this security breach and the sheep would stay within a pen. So they started shredding with lack-luster gusto. The USAID chief, still optimistic, feared jail time once a Congressional probe discovered the millions of dollars squandered on shuttered school buildings, agricultural instruction or infrastructure improvement.

Furthermore, he had no answer for the pallets, yes, pallets, of cash that were flown into Iraq on a regular basis for years. Shrink-wrapped in plastic, the printing-press fresh greenbacks were distributed via manila envelopes and accounted for on hand-receipts. Bits of paper signed by semi-literate Iraqis who promised to help realize the dream of democracy, a transformed Middle East, a westernized-Mesopotamia.

Baghdad's CIA station chief had no such woes. The Agency was slow, but not stupid. After the Tehran debacle most off-shore records were placed on hard drives or removable electronic storage. Emergency destruct was relatively easy in these cases.

Until the April 2001 EP-3 landing on Hainan Island. Damaged in a collision with an intercepting Chinese fighter, the intelligence collection platform had set down on a People's Liberation Army airfield—a decision derided within the Beltway, where the "true" intelligence community felt the pilot should have crashed into the ocean. Too late for hindsight. The Chinese, and presumably everyone else, now knew how to recover data from supposedly scrambled storage devices.

So CIA migrated to the NSA-devised "cloud." Encryption that could not be broken without causing byte self-destruction. The intel staffers simply went offline and smashed their machines. All files gone in less than 20 minutes.

The visa office made USAID look like paradise—a single commercial shredder that left strips eerily similar to those taped together by Iranian amateurs in 1979. Comprised of low-level State staffers and cheap foreign hires, the visa crew simply gave up and stuffed files into black garbage bags.

In the midst of this cascading failure, the RSO watched his authority literally going up in flames.

Ambassador Dumpty led a parade outside toward the housing area, his civilian flunkies ringed by a Marine security team led by the crusty E-7.

RSO could almost hear Dumpty's hoarse command:

"Burn it."

In his mind's eye, the RSO could see Marines pouring liberated diesel over the piles of files. He could hear the flash-bang grenades that would ignite the blaze, and he could smell the fire catching.

One problem solved. A paper mountain up in smoke.

Then there was the file system they could not burn. The pallets of USAID cash no one knew about.

Well, almost no one.

Alas, it was becoming clear the cash would not go to waste. The RSO put his hands over his eyes as he contemplated a new "evacuation plan" he and Ambassador Dumpty had just received from Washington.

The four Russian contract Il-76 crews were charging a million bucks per flight to Kuwait with their radioactive human cargo, not to mention free fuel from the airport bunkers. Cash, no paperwork.

Assuming, of course, the Ranger team could get them from the Green Zone to BIAP ahead of ISIS.

The Russians were there, all right, landing half an hour after the Rangers had. Whoever had controlled the airstrike on the airfield had taken out the entire ISIS advance force, purchasing valuable time— now they were going to buy the world's most expensive plane tickets.

The Russian pilots had one luxury the American and other Western flyboys could not indulge. They drank, before, during and after a flight. If the embassy people made it to BIAP, they could look forward to a terrifying emergency takeoff amid SAMs and machine gun fire, the giant Russian hulks lurching around the sky like their pilots, who were too drunk to stand.

Sounded like a hell of a plan. Not that there were any better ones.

BIAP – 42 HOURS AFTER EMBASSY DETONATION

Faheem and More drove onto the cargo ramp with the remaining Rangers in follow mode. No sense in heading for the ambassador until they knew transport arrangements were in place. The remaining USAF C-17 crews were all business. Weapons at ready, planes turned for rapid egress.

The Russians were anything but business. Dressed in stained jeans, hoodies and knock-off black leather jackets.

"Time to head downtown." More providing direction. Faheem was no longer the boss, he simply wore the rank.

Malaki was clearly pissed with the whole state of affairs. His remaining two armored Suburbans were trapped amidst a sea of decrepit Land Cruisers.

Their initial destination had been the Green Zone. Safety as far as the former Iraqi leader knew. Only to be swung around in a violent U-turn executed at a traffic circle. Right back to hell. The airport was a confusion of Islamic State snipers, Shia militia and a few Iraqi Security Force regulars trying to restore order. Add to that the sudden addition of American military professionals and the potential for being shot went well past the even mark.

Situation bad.

Faheem had no time or patience for the chaos.

Malaki could drop dead and not be missed. He certainly would not be mourned in Washington. But for the moment this Iraqi political hack was a valuable commodity. He had access to transportation assets. Including, now, the truck drivers who kept Baghdad supplied despite the insanity that existed between Jordan's borders and the

Euphrates River. A hardy lot who knew more about diesel engines than an American mechanic would learn in a lifetime, they lived by a simple slogan, "Where there is fear, there is money."

Malaki had plugged into the routing service. The trucks would cover whatever the buses could not haul. Some of the ambassador staff was going to be delivered to the airport in the back end of an eighteen-wheel semi stinking of old vegetables and rotting beef.

Faheem was too busy with security details to be gloating over the fate of State Department employees.

He had roughly 90 Rangers left at his disposal. And now he was missing at least three vehicles with men who were not likely to return—men who had seized ISIS vehicles left on the tarmac and then disappeared into chaos swirling about the airport complex. All of which had to be tallied into an equation that was supposed to result in rescuing 5,000 people from the dustiest, deadliest environment in the remnant of an ancient empire.

Forty of the Rangers were deployed as security for the sitting birds. Russian and American pilots were working out a deconfliction code for fear Iraqi air controllers would fail to transmit directions in a manner that would avoid runway accidents. The Russians, used to operating out of African airfields and other undesirable facilities, had it down in 10 minutes. Everything would be dependent on timing. Twenty minutes to "turn and burn." That meant the human cargo would be running onto airframes and not monitored for "buckling in."

The Russians didn't care. The Americans were learning there was little choice. USAF safety codes went into the circular file. Sometimes the second and third world has lessons to offer "civilized" society. Vodka for everyone sitting in a cockpit.

Was going to be a long night, sit back and enjoy your flight.

CHAPTER 13

ANKARA, TURKEY – 48 HOURS AFTER EMBASSY DETONATION

Gunay was swimming in a world of shit. Fikriye left a sequence of nasty messages on his cell phone—she felt abandoned and betrayed after three days of his unexplained absence from her bed. "Women," he muttered under his breath. Everything was about them, apparently forgetting that men sometimes played a useful function outside of the house.

His political bosses were no better. The phone rang incessantly with demands for updates on events within Baghdad. Educated guesses and truncated observations taken from media coverage were rapidly dismissed as "intelligence babble." They wanted answers and options for countering Washington's demands for humanitarian assistance. Oh that he were a clairvoyant or Roma fortune-teller. At least the pols would be willing to accept "best guesses" from those sources of wisdom.

And then there was Saeed. This diversion to rescue the remains of Suleiman Shah pulled his best operator out into Kurdistan for no obvious purpose other than to assist in Erdogan's ego trip. Yes, yes, it was about national pride—or so he had been informed in a phone call from the president's offices. Some lackey who sold the Turkish leader on the importance of myths, legacy and history. Heady stuff, if your ass was not on the line for recovering a bag of dusty bones.

Saeed, true to form, at least kept Gunay informed on his location and events unfolding in Rojava. Kurdistan was abuzz with rumors of how ISIS planned to proceed in the coming days and weeks. Many were afraid Baghdadi and Aboud were plotting a repeat of the fate that had befallen Mosul.

Mosul, a sad story that would pass into history like Babel and Ur.

A mere two years old, the new Caliphate had appeared about to lose possession of a prized bit of Iraqi territory, so Al-Baghdadi had turned to Hassan Aboud and let all ideas come to play. Aboud, never in danger of being accused of humanitarian tendencies, came up with an answer that would stun newspaper readers across the planet. He drowned an entire city.

For years Western reporters had warned that the Mosul Dam was a disaster waiting to happen. Constructed in 1984 by a consortium of German and Italian firms, the cement behemoth was a nightmare from the start. Ignoring geologist reports that the gypsum foundation would inevitably corrode, Saddam Hussein had poured money into European coffers—resulting in a structure that would flood the Tigris and all in that river's path.

It took nearly two tons of high explosives and over 150 good men, but Aboud managed to realize that nightmare.

He drowned Mosul and somewhere in the vicinity of 300,000 Iraqis—many Sunni.

Now the rumormongers were suggesting a similar fate for a much larger target. Perhaps even Tehran.

Gunay shrugged off this gossip. Sunni extremists were always seeking a means of disposing with Iran. No one was going to snuff out the ambitions of 78 million Persians that easily. Would take more than floods and a plague of locusts to depose the Iranian clerics. Gunay filed the apoplectic stories in a bank of his memory and returned to reviewing notes from Saeed's latest conversation.

A more timely rumor did catch Gunay's attention. The Americans were running a QRF out of Jordan. Now that was news. Jordanian-Turkish relations had been at a low ebb for almost two years. In a closed-door meeting with U.S. politicians in January 2016, Jordan's King Abdullah II accused Ankara of enabling the infiltration of Islamist terrorists into Europe and encouraging a "radical Islamic solution" to the crises in the Middle East. He also claimed Turkey was abetting Baghdadi's illicit export of oil and stoking the European refugee crisis to gain leverage over the European Union.

A private conversation that went viral after one of the attending American politicians saw fit to share his thoughts with a journalist desperate for material that would put her by-line back on the front page.

An act of journalistic "courage" cost Gunay much of his access to counterparts in the Jordanian intelligence services. A real shame, as the Jordanians had a much better finger on Syria's pulse than even Saeed could achieve. But what can you do when politicos want to pursue their own agendas? Say what you will, King Abdullah was a politico, one in search of American aid dollars and greater prestige in the Middle East.

All of which brought him back to Saeed's comments on events in Qatar. Here the rumors were almost beyond the bounds of fiction. According to Saeed's sources, Doha was enlarging its quest to scuttle Riyadh's sway over events in the region. Gunay knew the Emir was brutally disappointed with *Al Jazeera* and the Muslim Brotherhood. He also knew Qatar was not shy about playing its military cards where success seemed foreordained. What really worried him from Saeed's call was the possibility Doha was preparing to step up its game in the dark art of operational intelligence. Wet work, social media and cyber warfare.

Shit.

That sent him scrambling off to the SWIFT team. Time for a second look at the money trails coming and going from Doha. Perhaps, if he was lucky, the SWIFT monitors would be able to discern a sudden flow of cash to offshore bank accounts in all the most likely places—banks in the Caribbean and Switzerland. This was akin to searching for a needle in a haystack, but what other option? They still were unable to break the SWIFT encryption, leaving his analysts to track the message "externals" (the "to" and "when") of messages on the system. The truly valuable "internals" (what was said inside the messages) remained beyond grasp.

Gunay's trip to the SWIFT team's work spaces—no one talked about such issues on a phone—was interrupted by a courier dispatched from the signals/communications intercept office.

"Sir." A breathless bit of respect from a harried clerk. "My supervisor directed I hand this to you immediately."

Gunay unfolded the paper. A transcript of the panicked C-17 pilots over Baghdad. "When did this come in?"

"A little over eight hours ago, it took time for translation." At least this clerk knew how to answer basic questions.

So, Washington now had troops on the ground and likely airframes in place to evacuate the ambassador. (He would learn of the Il-76 landings from a communications intercept of the BIAP air traffic controllers a few hours later—a bit of data that only confirmed what he already had concluded: a desperate rescue attempt was under way.)

"Thank you." He dismissed the clerk and proceeded on to his SWIFT team. The Qatari angle was unnerving. If Doha was looking to weigh-in on this mess, who else in the region was looking to exert influence? And what would be the consequences for Turkey?

ANKARA, TURKEY – 48 HOURS AFTER EMBASSY DETONATION

Still disgruntled over his Suleiman Shah errand, Saeed had withheld a bit of news that might have really caught Gunay's attention. The Kurds were certain the American QRF in Jordan was operating in Syria—on a regular basis. Nothing that would capture attention. A snatch and grab or assassination here and there. Or so the rumors went. The Americans were well-trained, silent, and worked in close coordination with drones or aircraft. Seemingly traveled in and out of Jordan with ease, slipping security on both sides of the border.

One rumor stood out among the rest. The QRF had a team of "old hands" on board. A snippet that sent Saeed into deep thought. He knew of only a few "old hands" on the American side who still trod in his territory. The "elders" in U.S. intelligence operations tended to drift home to headquarters, a quiet desk job, and a renewed attempt at saving one's marriage or start a new family.

That, or they drank themselves to death or found some other form of self-destructive behavior less risky than being shot in unfriendly environs, but no less conducive to longevity.

Two faces almost immediately came to the fore. An aging Marine who spoke multiple languages and was obviously not just a Marine, and an Army major who Saeed had encountered while on a trip to Baghdad during the American occupation. This major spoke fluent Arabic and wore an SF tab above his Ranger insignia. This type does not simply retire to Washington, Saeed's only thought at the time.

His bet was that these two were back, with company, and likely headed for Baghdad.

He only spent a minute contemplating a follow-on thought— What kind of baggage did they bring with them? Such men acquire enemies and grudges like a bookseller draws musty texts.

Perhaps he should let Gunay in on this insight.

Perhaps.

CHAPTER 14

AMERICAN EMBASSY BAGHDAD – 48 HOURS AFTER DETONATION

Diplomacy is theater conducted on the privacy of very small stages. An office, limousine or park bench. There are no ethics in diplomacy, only mutually acceptable concessions. Neither party wins, nor does either side lose. It is a game of semantics that appeals to lawyers and political scientists; no worthy entrepreneur would engage in such malarkey.

Ambassador Dumpty had no time for such ruminations. He was now two days into a humanitarian crisis that was only going from bad to worse.

Despite his RSO's best efforts and stern comments to senior staffers, rumors of the peculiar nature of this attack were in complete circulation less than three hours after detonation. Thank God the State Department prohibited pregnant women from volunteering for hardship postings. But he still had to deal with a feisty lot of self-important career federal employees. This meant every eight hours he was compelled to provide an update briefing in the compound's auditorium.

Lord, he missed military-only audiences, they were polite and quiet.

State Department employees, on the other hand, acted as though they were back-benchers during "Question Time" at London's Palace of Westminster. His remarks would draw scoffs, catcalls and even an occasional boo. In this case it was panicked questions about evacuation, cursing about his incompetence, and demands he publically request Washington act to rescue. As one member of the audience so ably put it: "Shame the White House on TV for failing to act." And then there were the weepers. Sitting among their compatriots engaged in helpless sobs. The doomed, afraid to die.

Great advice if you had job security and a guaranteed pension. Dumpty was in possession of neither.

He hated every minute of stage time. And yet, had no recourse but to appear. Any whisper of his disappearing would only cause further panic and public outrage. A development the White House had made very, very, very clear, was unacceptable.

While the jihadi raid had shattered windows and spewed radiation, it had not severed the internet connection his over-paid IT contractors kept on-line come sun, rain or dust storms. Truck bombs, radiation poisoning—just another day in the life. As a result, his "fucking minions," the ambassador's exact words, wasted no time in contacting members of Congress and the press with news of this outrageous predicament. Less than five hours into his crisis, the Oval Office—or at least a representative claiming to speak for same—had called on a private line and issued one specific command: He would not leave the compound until every other American citizen was safely headed toward Baghdad's airport.

When he passed that tidbit along to his lawyer wife, the conversation went immediately downhill.

"They expect you to die in place like a disposable GS-9?" (Her derogatory way of referring to the federal government's pay structure—administrative assistants—"secretaries," back before everyone had a laptop—were GS-9s. He was far above such a lowly pay grade.)

"Yes, dear." Best answer he could offer, knowing Washington was monitoring his every communication.

"Grow a pair, and tell them no." She was now in full attorney mode. As best he could tell, law school was not just an education, it permanently warped expectations and perspectives. Lawyers all acted like the world owed them an answer. No wonder Shakespeare had recommended they be the first to die.

"I'm the ambassador, dear."

She knew this, of course, but perhaps needed a gentle reminder the title came with responsibilities. About 5,000 souls at the moment.

"You have a family here, and disposable grunts there to handle this kind of shit."

He could see the shared glances back in Washington when they read this transcript. His years atop the Foreign Service pecking order were shrinking to days and hours. Time to get her off the phone before any more damage was done.

"I love you."

He hung up before she could parry that one.

Women, can't live with them, can't live without them, and beatings were out of the question. This thought, as soon as it registered within his skull, was a dull reminder he had been in the Middle East much too long. No sane Western man would think beatings for a spouse were appropriate. Here, they were everyday affairs.

These unpleasant musings were interrupted by a sharp knock on the door. No need to guess who was standing outside his one escape from the unwashed masses—that Marine E-7 was back, inevitably with bad news.

"Come in." Spoken in a weary tone, perhaps a sign of exhaustion would slow down the NCO's "Energy Bunny" mode.

No such luck.

"Forward security is reporting a convoy of trucks and buses merging outside the perimeter walls." He meant the Emerald Zone, not the ambassador's own cloister, but the ambassador understood without need for requesting clarification.

"Really?" He let this one-word question escape with more than a bit of incredulity in his tone. "Despite the very public announcement of our radiation problem, the Iraqi drivers are willing to come here?"

The Marine did not miss a beat.

"Mr. Ambassador, money speaks even louder than concerns about personal health when you're starving. We're finally leaving. Malaki called in all his chips so we'll haul his ass out of here as we go."

"You *are* screening these vehicles before they pass through out gates? I'll have rioting if there are more bombings, on-board snipers or suicide idiots." A necessary question for the still running in-office recording devices—a post-Benghazi development.

"No."

Not the answer he wanted, but at least it was now on the record.

"Start the parade, one backpack-sized bundle per passenger. The rest of their shit stays here."

"What about weapons?" The NCO was covering every base.

"If they're wearing a U.S. military uniform, they go armed. Everyone else has to be trusted until we reach American soil." A quiet acknowledgement that many of his public servants were carrying guns that did not show up on an approval roster.

The NCO let that observation pass without comment. The RSO had already made clear his armed personnel would be "packing" when the vehicles rolled.

"Roger that Sir, going to be a lot of happy law enforcement types when we get home." The NCO's way of suggesting local cops and security at U.S. airports would just abscond with seized illegal weapons and then sell them on the black market. Welcome back to the good ol' U.S. of A.

"Any *good* news for me?" Dumpty's sarcasm was more than evident.

"No." The Marine sergeant locked heels, gave a sharp salute and left.

Leadership is a lonely profession riddled with opportunities for failure. Ambassador Dumpty hated his job.

BIAP – 48 HOURS AFTER DETONATION

Less than 10 miles to the west, Major Faheem was in an equal shit storm. The Pentagon's "gift" of para-dropped Army Rangers was nothing to dismiss. They had, after all, cleared the runway of rabid "ragheads" and provided safe landing rights for the Russian Candids. Faheem knew shit about flying a plane, but he was impressed with what the Russian pilots pulled off.

Apparently oblivious to tracer rounds and occasional shoulder-fired rocket-propelled grenades, these travel-worn aircrews dumped cargo jets on tarmac at a pace that exhausted the Iraqi runway service personnel, and also quickly suggested a shortage of armed guards sufficient to prevent an attack that could cause a domino effect in exploding fuel tanks.

The trick to solving this problem, as Faheem had been informed, was to locate aircraft at parking spaces such that one disaster did not trigger multiple other "bad" events. For instance, one plane burns, explodes, and sets the adjacent airframe on fire. The domino effect. Easy to see happening in a crowded passenger terminal—he wondered why the jihadi assholes hadn't tried this at O'Hare or LAX yet.

Baghdad's control tower crew was better than their American counterparts. Bad shit happened here all the time, precaution was also known as survival. Aircraft were parked at every *other* gate.

Problem mitigated, but not solved.

What most civilians—hell, most military officers—do not understand is that no runway or taxi area at an airport is constructed to sustain long-term parking of a large aircraft (anything over six hours). The very fact these flying beasts typically rest on just three contact points with mother earth meant the probability of sinking through asphalt and even cement was high.

To prevent such disasters, "parking ramps" or "hard points" were built into runway layouts and storage areas. Each parking ramp came with a load rating and there were only a precious few—all the required rebar and cement for one of these ramps was damned expensive.

Not that airports did not figure out how to recover the costs.

Parking a 747 at Tokyo's Narita Airport cost $1,000 an hour.

Military airbases were less expensive, but much harder to access.

The Candid crews were crowding out available parking space until the ambassador got their asses in gear.

Faheem started making unpleasant calls. The first went to Ambassador Dumpty's RSO.

"Where the fuck are my passengers?"

The RSO knew how to handle a pissed-off Army major, but bit his tongue.

"Waiting your 'all clear.'"

Great, Faheem quietly sighed to himself, now they were setting the stage for more blame-games. He had an emergency evacuation to pull off under fire, and this prick was worrying about Congressional hearings back home down the road—*if* they survived.

"We're ready." Faheem's terse response.

He was lying. They hadn't secured Route Irish, just the airport.

"Roger, we'll begin loading and transport." The line went dead.

Now the real fun began.

AMERICAN EMBASSY BAGHDAD – 48.5 HOURS AFTER DETONATION

"Bring the buses in first."

Figuring the ambassador wanted his coterie of State Department seniors taken out on round one, the RSO requested the most comfortable transport options be allowed prioritized access.

The rank and file could be piled into semi-truck trailers, but this collection of stuffed shirts and skirts would cause endless pain if not treated with kid gloves. So, onto the handful of air-conditioned buses they went. Bitching and moaning the entire time about having to leave behind prized possessions.

He could never figure out why people brought so much personal crap to a war zone. A long-time bachelor—marriage three had cured his interest in anything other than a dog living beneath the same roof—he found little interest in knickknacks and dust collectors. The only reason pictures adorned his office was an administrative assistant who felt the bare spaces were too reminiscent of a prison. She found a batch of "happy snaps" in the Public Affairs section and requested they be framed and hung appropriately.

"Looks like Goebbels's workspace." His response to her efforts.

No one would ever accuse him of being soft-hearted.

Sentimental senior civil servants toted stuffed backpacks aboard the buses and demanded someone inventory their abandoned spaces as a means of accounting for lost treasures. The RSO did not share his intention to burn everything remaining upon their departure—by U.S. Marines or air strike, didn't matter. This jihadi radiation was not going to be shipped back to *his* country, at least not via "humanitarian" deliveries from a surrendered American embassy.

Six buses with 56 seated passengers and 10 more sitting in the aisles—396 about to roll out the gates. Only 4,600 more to go. This was going to be a long fucking day.

A sentiment shared by Marines assigned to escort this tranche of passengers to BIAP.

Up-armored Humvees did not mean air-conditioned Humvees. Nor did it render one invulnerable to snipers or idiots lobbing cement slabs off the bridges spanning Route Irish. Add to this a none-too-subtle fact they had to come back after every drop-off at the airport terminal, and you had statistical odds that very much favored the Grim Reaper.

Nonetheless, there was no shortage of willing volunteers. Twenty-year-olds with a lust for thrills and an opportunity to kill at will were plentiful within the Corps.

Loaded aboard four Humvees with five-man teams (women were now "men" in the U.S. Marine Corps), they came with a driver, three street-level guns and a manned roof-turret .50 cal. Not much the jihadi could throw in their way with rolling stock. The hardest trick was keeping the Iraqi bus drivers from separating by more than 15 feet.

Made for nerve-wracking driving skills, but that way no vehicle would slip into their convoy—and the buses were easily corralled by the Humvees. This was textbook or field-manual perfect execution. The passengers could now sit back and relax. The Marines were doing same, but in their own way. What the Humvees lacked in air-conditioning was more than compensated for by modern communications systems.

The Bluetooth comm gear was dialed right into an auxiliary jack that made available every iPod a jarhead could smuggle into country. Leadership may have frowned upon loud rock, but there was little that could be done to discourage this practice. Besides, some form of distraction was better than strung out kids coming back from 10 hours of stressed-filled "fun" on the IED-laden roads of Iraq.

The jihadi made driving an act of willful suicide. No reason to begrudge the kids their music. "Load and Rock," was a common phrase for every team departing a safe enclave.

AMERICAN EMBASSY BAGHDAD – 50 HOURS AFTER DETONATION

Install all the glass and sound absorption you want, nothing completely defeats that diesel turnover—a start-up noise truck drivers likened to money about to happen, and soldiers equated with letters to wives and parents that no one wanted to receive.

The lead Humvee rolled out though a debris field once known as Al-Baghdadi's Truck Nine with no hesitation. If there was a second thought, it sure as hell was not coming out of this team. Nor the second or third escort. There might have been second thoughts in the trail vehicle—lead or trail were first to die, always place the insane in front. Trail had to think about what was going to happen in front and behind. At least the lead had comfort in knowing everyone else was an arriving cavalry. Trail had to wonder how long it would take distracted team members to turn around and circle the wagons. Woe to be trail.

No one asked the Iraqi bus drivers what they thought.

Iraqi men had been at war since September 1980, when Saddam Hussein decided it was time to wreak havoc on the Shia apostates in Iran. There was no equivalent of an American Veterans Administration in Baghdad. As an Iraqi you licked the wounds, dusted off plaster, buried dead children, and then went on trying to scrape out a living.

AMERICAN EMBASSY BAGHDAD – 50.5 HOURS AFTER DETONATION

Aboud Hassan knew the buses were rolling less than five minutes after the first engine started. His watchers were buried into the west side of Baghdad in a manner that would have made Saddam proud. He knew when a new shop opened, when a bricklayer quit his job to join a militia, and, certainly, what passed through the portals of Rome's Emerald City. His phone rang as soon as the second bus driver fired up his diesel.

He sat back—secure in an undisclosed safe house--and awaited the next call.

Even in a world of IEDs and sloppy executions, timing was everything.

It took the Marine lead and trail and a sandwiched bus convoy 15 minutes to clear the Emerald City's outer perimeter and enter Route Irish.

Now the cell phone calls were coming in at 30-second increments. Just simple voice messages.

"Marker 1.2."

Kilometer measurements he made each watcher memorize. When the lead Humvee passed their position all he required was that statement. Better than texting; nervous hands made for misplaced numeric references.

Oh, he knew this mode of data relay was more susceptible to intercept, but by the time Americans at NSA figured out what was about to happen his work would be done.

"Marker 2.3."

The job had been done, explosives were in place, and not a drone in sight.

"Marker 3.7."

Less than 70 seconds. Hassan would have been pacing the room if his legs were still attached. Too much was riding on this gambit for a cripple to simply stir about on a wheelchair. Too late for such considerations. Al-Baghdadi was going to have his demands answered in a single event. He offered a silent 15 seconds to Allah.

"Marker 5.3."

AMERICAN EMBASSY BAGHDAD – 50.75 HOURS AFTER DETONATION

The blast was loud enough to drown out all the human shuffling within Ambassador Dumpty's world. The Emerald City went silent before a dust or smoke plume was visible. A blast of that magnitude only meant one thing—bad karma.

There was no need for the Marine NCO or RSO reports. He knew Route Irish was now closed. His wife would be pissed, and then checking their life insurance policies. Another side of legal training he found abhorrent—leave no small stone unturned. She had demanded he take out at least $5 million on his own head before leaving for Baghdad. Looks like the children would be going to an expensive private school after all.

Two calls to make.

His line to the State Department watch went through in one ring. "Contact the secretary. ... NOW."

Call two, the White House situation room.

"Get the president on line—tell him the shit's hit the fan."

All this clamor, before anyone even knew what had transpired on Route Irish.

Right on cue, the Marine NCO and RSO burst into the office. Dumpty was too numb to be surprised.

"Want to tell me what's happened?"

Blank stares from both men standing opposite his desk.

"Let me guess, it isn't good."

More blank stares.

Dumpty managed a single order. "Contact BIAP command now."

Here, finally, were orders the NCO and RSO could execute. Both spun for the door, headed to their respective teams.

Ambassador Dumpty took no such action. He simply reached down to the lowest left drawer in his desk and pulled out a bottle of Jameson Irish Whiskey, one bar glass, and poured a long drink. No one was going home tonight. Or tomorrow.

CHAPTER 15

DOHA, QATAR – 50.75 HOURS AFTER DETONATION

Reminiscing, a luxury the Qatari defense minister allowed himself during long days behind a desk scattered with expenditures and personnel requests.

Today he was fondly recalling warm days in Colorado with his American counterparts. The last cast of a day spent fly-fishing is always the best. A light rod tip flicks back with a precision honed over six hours of practice, lure travels in intended direction, and the line—always prone to tangling—smoothly flows behind. With any luck there would be fresh trout roasting over a campfire 30 minutes later.

With any luck.

It was obvious to the defense minister that ODIN did not believe in luck, nor would he find much joy in fly-fishing. Too damn slow for such a man and not much to speak for at the end of a day of puddling about in cold water. Fly-fishing was an avocation for men who lost their bearings or claimed to need some time away from a daily grind.

As best he could tell, this ODIN was a one-day-at-a-time person. In his world there was no "daily grind." Each dawn brought new opportunities to succeed or die. Qatar's relatively open access for news feeds originating in the West—outgrowth of the Emir's sponsorship of *Al Jazeera*—meant the defense minister was up-to-date on Baghdad developments, and likely well ahead of the U.S. intelligence community.

The problem was "deluge"—as opposed to "systematic." Without his intelligence analysts, he was left to discern what sources should be filtered out of the inbox before information over-flow muddied decision making. Sifting wheat from chaff was no mean undertaking.

Dredging though the Web for value beyond a few remaining reputable media sources took skill and patience. One needed to learn the author's credentials and then discern his or her ability to acquire insiders with real knowledge. Your best bet was individuals who chose to share data for ethical reasons, intellectual satisfaction, and/or a sense of social contribution.

At least this much his intelligence team was able to learn about ODIN. First, he was a man with cash and intellectual moxie. The Qatari security services were able to learn his Dark Web email account pulled in 150–400 hits a day.

Oh, they had quickly learned of the Dark Web. Lessons dictated by the Emir's fear that this gateway would be used to challenge his leadership much as had been done in Bahrain, Egypt and even Iran.

As the IT geeks explained it to the defense minister, the Dark Web was a back channel conjured into existence by the U.S. Naval Research Lab. Yes, U.S. government employees, who discovered a means of employing thousands of free servers to route encrypted messages in a manner that largely rendered the sender or receiver untraceable. It employed Tor—"The onion router" (this was a capitalization format demanded by the protocol's designers, with no explanation; perhaps they were just tired of standard military abbreviations)—which made for a perfect means of conducting illegal business and passing sensitive information.

Which his chosen American operative apparently used with ease.

To make matters worse, financial transactions on Tor were all done in Bitcoin—a currency with no official government backing, but that had won a place on the international financial exchange in 2017. The *New York Times* and *Wall Street Journal* provided a daily conversion rate for Bitcoin against all major monetary denominations. And, he had learned, ODIN played the markets.

Just two hours after ODIN's meeting with the Emir, the defense minister was now endlessly pinging the reticent American. Qatar was going into the game with IT, not kinetics or the endless cash that belonged to Riyadh.

BIAP – 50.75 HOURS AFTER EMBASSY DETONATION

Funny thing about "No-Such-Agency"—a joke from 1974—regardless of movie plots from Hollywood, the NSA had no access to "enforcement agents." Neither More nor Faheem acted in response to NSA orders.

NSA existed to steer operations, not kill people. A shame, really, as passing NSA-collected data from one government agency to another simply delayed a timely response to perishable information.

In fact, the resulting time-lag was all in a clever adversary's advantage.

Sometimes.

Time lag could not incorporate what was about to happen to the evacuation caravan on Route Irish. That would have required a crystal ball, fortune cookie, or an imagination. The U.S. intelligence community had plenty of crystal balls (or the plastic eight-ball equivalent) and fortune cookie postings—it lacked imagination.

Aboud won the imagination game when the third ambassador evacuation bus crossing Caliph Baghdadi's tunnel under Route Irish split in two, gratis of a small fortune expended on high-explosives. Washington DC's current caretakers would lose the 2020 election. No constituency in a democracy reelects officials who sacrifice 4,500 American lives.

Exactly what Qatar wanted without knowing how it would

happen. Serendipity occurs, even for a royalty more known for depending on divine inspiration and an expenditure of large fortunes.

Allah sometimes appears in the form of crazed jihadi willing to sacrifice life and limb in the name of bringing forth the Muslim version of a Second Calling. What had just happened beneath Route Irish was a Second Calling. An opportunity to banish the Crusaders from Baghdad and bring an end to Washington's drone campaign.

Imagination was now the only way to conduct operations.

BIAP – 50.8 HOURS AFTER DETONATION

There was no missing what had just transpired. The detonation rocked all of Baghdad and blew debris over half a mile in any direction from Aboud Hassan's tunnel rats. It left the diggers deaf, but not dead. That job would be up to the surviving elements of Ambassador Dumpty's Marine security element. Sheltered from the worst by up-armored vehicles, that Marine team was already scrambling to win position on a battlefield littered with shattered cement and scattered asphalt—further decorated by remnants of two buses and their contents.

Journalists rarely provide vivid descriptions of how the human body disassembles when interrupted by high explosives.

In the bluntest polite terms, when explosively extinguished, human life comes apart. Limbs sever and scatter, heads have an odd tendency to roll off in a bowling ball trajectory, and internal organs splatter any flat surface. This "mural" is gruesome enough to cause battle-hardened medics immediate stomach upset. The young troops in Ambassador Dumpty's lead security vehicles were not medics— they puked all over the inside of already overheated vehicle interiors.

And that was before they started to discover survivors.

The dead are dead. Wounded missing limbs are shrieking disasters begging a final pistol shot.

No such option in the Western world.

But for the moment there was no time to contemplate triage or search and rescue. All the Marines knew was that someone had blown a huge trench in Route Irish and that they now had to establish a security perimeter sufficient for providing their own protection and preserving occupants of the two buses on their side of the blast site. The lone vehicle at the rear of this convoy was on its own.

That's when the sniper fire commenced.

After two decades of insurgent campaigns, this latest development was hardly unexpected. The jihadi were resilient, and occasionally imaginative, but when it came to on-scene developments—well, the remnant sniper was guaranteed—waiting to take out any Roman willing to exit an armored vehicle.

This sniper was less kind.

He or she began by shooting bombing survivors who exited a bus or screamed too loudly while bleeding out on the highway.

With an effectiveness that impressed the Marine staff sergeant charged with leading this security detail.

Single blasts suggesting a Russian-manufactured Dragunov sniper rifle—used a 7.62x54mm cartridge, longer than the AK-47's 7.62x39mm, but that added length meant it was a hell of a lot more effective at the 800-meter range that kept a killer out of sight.

Made a distinctive sound. And meant the Marines were not in a hurry to get out of their vehicles—screaming victims on the cement could wait. Why become another casualty?

An ugly scene with all the makings of an old-fashioned turkey shoot, save one modern innovation. The bus convoy had left with its own drone coverage. The boys in Idaho flying the death birds were about to have fun.

Sniper one went up in a wall of flames—the Hellfire is an aptly named missile.

Sniper two was no luckier.

The Marines were now out of their trucks and on the tarmac.

Buses one and two were still operable. Barely. Running on flat rear tires, the second bus was not going anywhere fast, but moving was better than awaiting another shooter. Bus three was a complete loss—and no one was willing to loiter in plain sight on an open high-way to consider the fate of the dead or dying.

"MOVE, MOVE, MOVE, FUCKING NOW!"

No failing to comprehend those instructions from the staff ser-geant. At least two cargo loads of bureaucrats were going to reach BIAP. The Marine NCO had no idea how to handle what remained. Leave that problem to eyes in the sky and forces that could reach out from the contaminated embassy compound.

What he didn't expect was the sudden appearance of four Toyota Land Cruisers flying American flags. Or the load of uniformed U.S. Rangers rolling out of the doors and back deck.

More and Faheem never made the ambassador—too fucking dan-gerous with all the jihadi and Sunni sympathizers blasting away. But the RSO had done his job—coordinates and travel speeds relayed be-fore the busses left for BIAP. The cavalry was late—late was still better than never. At least 120 Americans—alive, dead or wounded—were getting aboard planes. The remaining 4,800—now there was a differ-ent problem.

DOHA, QATAR – 50.8 HOURS AFTER DETONATION

Phone calls from the Emir's offices were never a good thing. Pleasant news was delivered in person or by email via a secure server. The de-fense minister had three such calls in less than five minutes.

"Get your American on site." End of conversation.

As best he could tell, ODIN boarded the Lear in an equally shitty mood.

Fuck those fly fishermen.

CHAPTER 16

AR-RAQQAH, CALIPHATE – 51.5 HOURS AFTER EMBASSY DETONATION

For Al-Baghdadi (aka Caliph Ibrahim) time had come to a halt. Aboud Hassan had gone incommunicado 20 minutes after the Islamic State's leader had been told the Roman's convoy on Route Irish was a funeral pyre. Long ago he had learned to ignore lackeys and supplicants who arrived with news complimentary of his objectives. This word he wanted to hear from the mouth of a man entrusted with meeting a much broader objective—rebirth of their Islamic Empire.

Historians contend the Umayyad Caliphate reached any imaginable height of "Prophet Mohammed's" ambition. An empire that stretched from areas east of modern Iran to the very gates of current France. Jesus Christ could make no such claim in A.D. 750 … and he had been dead for over seven hundred years. Prophet Mohammed was only in his grave for slightly more than a century when this achievement occurred.

Islam and its Caliph were nothing to be fucked with. The Spanish Inquisition was a two-bit player in contrast to the manner in which a Caliph in Damascus could deliver hell-fire upon an adversary in Europe of the Dark Ages. What Rome had wrought, Western ignorance was quickly forgetting and undoing.

He knew the numbers all too well. Aside from the Israelis, Western immigrants and Iranians—who were little more than Westerners with a touch of Arabic blood—the new caliphate was ostensibly devoid of forward thinking. His potential flock accounted for less than one percent of global patent applications filed in a single year. And most of that feeble number was explained by offshore companies operating in Saudi Arabia or Egypt seeking to protect their expatriate employees' intellectual efforts.

The same was true of academic debate and discussion of his cherished Koran. Baghdadi could offer but two dozen authoritative texts produced in the last three decades that caused philosophical arguments about the Prophet's words. And he was Sunni—a "Protestant" in the Islamic world. Allah only knew what feeble conversation took place among the Shia apostates.

Finally came education and employment.

While many governments in his caliphate claimed literacy rates above 80 percent, that figure was based on polling of males and used a very loose definition of ability to read and write. Factor in women and then add a clause known as "functional and employable"—literacy decidedly dropped below 50 percent for most of the region.

He smiled at this thought. No surprise the Roman bid to compel democracy in Iraq failed. Constituents seeking to install a functional government via elections needed to be able to read.

As for employment. Despite ready access to ports and close proximity to consumer markets (Europe and the United States), manufacturers shunned the Middle East, choosing instead higher transportation costs from Asia and India. Reason one: little faith in Middle Eastern political stability. Reason two: a work force that thought five sessions of daily prayer and going on leave for a month every year for Ramadan were viable business practices.

All of which meant that literacy and college education were wasted on a youth who could not find work and thereby afford marriage. Young educated men without jobs are future jihadi—so are young women in the same situation. If you know how to read and can compare your situation to those of a similar age outside this miserable region; well, revolution in the name of Allah seems an all-too appropriate solution.

This would change with his caliphate, but first the Romans must go, and with them the cursed Iranians.

So he awaited news from Baghdad.

AL MAYADIN, NORTHEAST FORMER SYRIA – 51.5 HOURS AFTER EMBASSY DETONATION

Hassan Aboud was in a shitty mood. Hunkered down outside a village on the eastern outskirts of former Syria, he was watching a gunfight play out between erstwhile Arab Spring remnants and his less-than-proficient guardians. A well-read man, despite his humble upbringing, he had no argument with historians who suggested the crusaders prevailed because Arab men were unable to muster the courage to die in direct contact with an adversary.

His current predicament was evidence history had not changed. Standing behind five-foot-high walls, the adversaries simply lay their AK-47s on the top of said enclosures and sprayed bullets at each other. No casualties or consequences other than chipped paint and a few dead dogs.

There was no telling what he would pay for foreign mercenaries willing to aim and expend ammunition in a sparing manner. Aboud privately admired the fire discipline and accuracy of Western military opponents; his troops were far from such proficiency.

Fortunately, his adversaries—at least if they were Iraqi or Iranian—were little better. Life only became miserable when Romans appeared. Then shit hit the fan.

Aboud was worrying about that very development as he watched the scene in front of him unfold.

Washington may have cared little about Syrian civilian casualties, but the bastards at CIA missed no opportunity to use drones for killing idiots exchanging fire in the open. All it would take was one cell phone call or an explosion with significant infrared signature to draw the silent birds of death. Then he and his men would be little more than carrion feed—blasted about the desert by drone-launched missiles that seemingly never missed. It was time to get out of this mess.

A logical observation, but missing a single, essential means for accomplishing such an escape. Vehicles, even when "camouflaged" with roof-top markings used on Western transport equipment, drew attention in the former Syrian-Iraqi border region. A drone pilot, with good reason, paid no end of attention to anything moving west-to-east. Those cars and trucks were likely loaded with jihadi or supplies headed for the front line.

Anything headed west was either fleeing civilians or bearing wounded. Both were off the Roman target list. As a result, Aboud feared little heading west. Driving east was a whole different conversation.

"Start shifting men 1,000 meters to the south." His first command passed via a runner—yes, a human trotting back and forth—to the local commander.

"Once to the enemy's left flank move men 100 meters past their forward firing position." He was setting up an L-shaped ambush.

"Refrain from firing until everyone is in position." An attempt to use surprise.

So the ruse began—with unusual effectiveness—at least if judged by the Pentagon's standards. Aboud's forces—at the senior end—rivaled U.S. counterparts in experience and tradecraft, even without extensive field manuals and formal military education. Schools teach theory, hands-on participation makes a soldier.

The ambush maneuver worked like magic. Would-be democracy advocates melted away to ruins and sewer tunnels as their colleagues died around them. No time for body counts, celebrity gunfire or looting of the dead, he had to keep rolling. News from Baghdad required confirmation and a fluid adjustment of forces if the effect was to have long-term consequences.

Travel along the remnants of highways scarred by bombs, rocks and wrecks were always hazardous, more so when the pock-marked asphalt was adrift in dust and drivers feared drone strikes. Conditions resulting in security convoys that were not remotely secure. His protective detail allowed two or three other vehicles to get between lead and trail teams. The consequence was a less observable force, but one that left him vulnerable.

But not nervous.

Fear is an irrational emotion.

A sentiment he espoused for years, despite the loss of his two legs and numerous soldiers. Fear, he knew, was actually quite rational. It prevented men from committing to acts that might result in their own bodily harm or death.

An absence of fear did not equate to a lack of planning. Aboud was more than cognizant of the fact that his decision to rain horrors upon the Roman escape attempt was going to draw hell from above. Despite innumerable attempts to shut down drone support bases or jam software communications, the Americans kept death from the sky an operational option.

Only the Iranians had succeeded in hacking through the command codes—and that success was good for exactly one intercept. Then the bastards switched to yet another means of controlling their pilotless bats.

Some things must be accepted as inevitable obstacles. Drones were one. Suicide bombers were another.

Aboud had no qualms about dispatching men and women to die in the name of jihad. Over the years his chemists and explosive engineers had become superbly adept at crafting devices that all-but defied detection. Surgery to implant the required C-4 and detonator took but a few hours. Simply dial the right number on a ubiquitous cell phone—and, sudden chaos.

Aboud was now prepared to take the tactical advantage of bombing the embassy and destroying Route Irish to the strategic level of warfare.

The idea was very simple—strategic employment was more difficult.

At the outset you had to convince a young man or woman it was time to die in the name of a greater cause. Insert appropriate explosive device and the stage was set. But where one executed the explosive was a dicier proposition. Long gone were the days when a bus, café or restaurant caused emotional stress for an adversary. Iraqis, Israelis, Libyans Syrians and Turks had long ago acquiesced to the idea that a public outing could be fatal.

Now the targets were selected for political impact in Berlin, Paris and Washington. Strike a day care center, elementary school, hospital emergency room or police training compound—then there were headlines and a sense of panic in the general population.

Aboud went for the vulnerable and relished the consequences. Baghdad was about to learn that in a painful manner.

Less than 20 minutes after the Route Irish detonation, suicide bombers struck a day care catering to Iraq's Ministry of the Interior, five emergency response wards, and an outdoor market in Sadr City. Initial casualty estimates ran to the hundreds.

Making life—or death—even more miserable, his technology wizards shut down police and fire communications networks. Let the games begin. A few snipers thrown in the midst, well, death could come from the street level as effectively as it came from above.

Looking at his watch he realized it was time to reach back to Ar-Raqqah. The Caliph needed to be updated. Communications to outside parties were necessary for the party to continue.

AR-RAQQAH – 51.8 HOURS AFTER EMBASSY DETONATION

Cell phones, smart phones, whatever. Al-Baghdadi felt the damned device come to life before it actually rang. Hollywood script writers had tipped him to the fact that an unintended cell phone ring could be fatal—so he left the devices on vibrate. With a 30-second delay before it could emit noises that might draw unwanted attention.

Aboud, as ever, was abrupt and off the line.

"Steps one and two accomplished." End of conversation.

Step three was going to be brutal.

In almost every society there is an innate desire to assist injured and dying. Men and women reach out to strangers in ways they never would if the victim were still standing and apparently healthy. Aboud was no psychologist, but he knew how to inflict pain on good Samaritans. Wait for 10 minutes, and then execute a second attack on the site of his initial mayhem.

Ten minutes was not accidental—although it proved convenient for training semi-literate operatives. Even they could be taught to read a digital watch and then react. It seemed strange that law and military authorities never inculcated a delay function into alert response times—perhaps it was a bid to win public support. As for the civilian rescuers—family or simply uninjured by-standers—well, 10 minutes gave them time to watch dust clear, regain hearing lost to an explosion, and gather bearings.

The next set of attacks went exactly as planned—outdoor markets littered with bodies and limbs thanks to a troupe of suicide bombers; countless police stations ablaze and multiple Shia mosques rendered unapproachable due to sniper fire.

Baghdad was now a city in panic.

Aboud made one more call to Ar-Raqqah.

"It is done." Enough said.

Al-Baghdadi smiled.

CHAPTER 17

There is a Western saying that argues home is simply where one chooses to rest your head. Home, the Qatari defense minister was certain, did not include a battered Toyota diesel Land Cruiser bouncing across hard packed red dust in southern Iraq. His American passenger looked no less displeased.

Death from above had no appeal for the defense minister, and yet, here he was, chauffeuring some psychotic American across the open desert in plain sight of manned aircraft and drones. A passenger who issued constant terse demands he drive faster, thus causing an even greater trail of dust for the pilots to follow.

ODIN appeared not to give a shit about his driver's concerns. He was operating on instructions passed from Aboud—loyalty to the highest bidder always is in best interest of a would-be mercenary— by-passing the Qatari leadership. He was now insistent they make Hadithah as soon as possible.

Rumor was that much of the ISIS leadership was now holed up in this village of 25,000 located along the Euphrates River. A strange development, as the locale sat beneath the Hadithah dam and had supposedly been under Baghdad's control since 2015.

Unlike Mosul, al-Baghdadi had spared Hadithah. The dam above this collection of semi-paved streets and one-room family stores had been left to slumber. Hadithah was settled and peaceable. Any war damage was rapidly reconstructed; a relatively simple process given the unpainted cinderblock homes that characterized architecture throughout Iraq, Jordan, Lebanon and Syria. Nondescript square one- or two-story flat-roofed structures surrounded by an eight-foot-tall cinderblock wall so as to ward off thieves, corral chickens, and stow a collection of abused vehicles.

Hassan Aboud was less concerned about death from above than ensuring his next move received proper support. A pool of youth ready to die in the name of Allah was an effective weapon when dealing with Iraqi or Syrian conscripts. They were painfully ineffective when the Americans or Iranians stepped in.

Thus an outreach to Qatar. Doha was no natural ally. The Emir fiscally and physically supported a moderate voice for Islam—the Muslim Brotherhood. And then went in search of a means of by-passing the House of Saud.

But how?

The answer arrived with ISIS. Suddenly there was an opportunity to seize, even if it meant negotiating with extremists. The Emir leapt at his chance—pouring cash into "charities" that competed with Al Waqf al Islam, a Saudi-based funding source that first distributed cash in the Balkans and then expanded across the Levant. Given a chance to turn the tide on Wahhabism, Doha did not miss a beat.

So why dispatch ODIN to Hadithah? Why not leave this man in Doha under close supervision?

Hadithah, Aboud assured his Qatari contacts, came with a stench the Americans were unwilling to inhale. He reminded them of November 2005, when a team of U.S. Marines massacred 24 Iraqi noncombatants "in cold blood," or so the event was characterized by a former member of Congress.

The Marine squad leader was charged with manslaughter and his senior officer faced reprimand for dereliction of duty. Suddenly, shades of Vietnam and the My Lai massacre hung heavily over George

Bush's war. Americans were not going near Hadithah, for fear of having to relive an already brutal lesson on history repeating itself.

It took Aboud some effort to pass this argument on to al-Baghdadi, but when it sunk in, things began to happen. Qatari funding became a source of cash to assist in rebuilding. The villagers abandoned any ties to Baghdad, and Iraqi conscripts quietly fled south. Hadithah now belonged to the Caliphate. And its nondescript homes became shelter from American drones.

What Aboud did not share with al-Baghdadi was the construction of a communications center in the heart of Hadithah. Here, via landline, ran a patchwork of microwave dishes and access to satellite-fed internet connections. ODIN was about to take over a new operations hub.

Quiet rumors of Caliphate and al-Qaeda ambitions to seize nuclear weapons from Pakistan had swirled through the Western intelligence community for years. Beset by social strife, economic disparity and a resident Taliban population, Islamabad's collection of atomic arms worried Washington policy makers into a tizzy of hearings and finger pointing.

The same thoughts had not occurred with Tehran's budding nuclear program, until the Iranians tested their first bomb.

Despite the best efforts of Israel's Mossad—assassinating Iranian nuclear scientists—or NSA's cyber campaign—Stuxnet caused the destruction of at least one-fifth of Iran's nuclear centrifuges via a malicious computer code—Tehran prevailed.

The so-called cessation agreement brokered with the UN Security Council permanent members and Germany only put a Band-aid on the problem, and reopened Iran's access to cash via oil sales. Took another three years, but the Ayatollah and Islamic Revolutionary Guard Corps were then prepared to send a message to Jerusalem, Riyadh and Washington—fuck with us and we will nuke you.

An above-ground test ensured all the interested parties understood what Iran had accomplished. Infrared sensors caught the blast from above and seismic collectors culled data from below. The Iranians had not squandered time—Tehran's first test confirmed enriched pluto-nium, with an estimated 10-megaton yield.

Diplomatic reaction was predictable—anger, hand-wringing and woe. Military responses were nonexistent—Israel and Saudi Arabia were directed to leave their aircraft on the ground. Pakistan cheered, North Korea lauded Tehran's courage.

Enter ODIN.

Concerned that NSA bureaucrats would wince at the thought of congressional oversight, the White House sought help from the private sector.

ODIN offered the Pentagon an out.

He crafted Operation Nitro Zeus, a campaign to disable Iran's air defenses, communications, and critical elements of the national power grid. Working with a team of geeks clothed in T-shirts, dirty jeans and canvas sneakers, he directed emplacement of software bots on multiple servers across Tehran's domain. They even tested, shutting down all Iran's internet access for eight hours one night, then blinding Iranian air defense on another. Feats accomplished from a small office building parked amidst the genteel neighborhoods of McLean, Virginia.

All done with no public complaint from Tehran, nor an attempt to hack into his servers. CIA's cyber security gurus, on the other hand, were inundated with Iranian counterattacks, as were the kids at Cyber Command. The attacks ranged from denial of service to flagrant front door electronic "explosives" mass emailed to CIA employees.

Aboud had far more ambitious plans for ODIN. He did not only want Iranian air defense and air control systems to go blind, he wanted Tehran's access to international banking channels to go silent—for a full week.

Shutting down SWIFT—the Society for Worldwide Interbank Financial Telecommunication—was a proven concept. Hackers, in 2016, had managed to steal over $80 million from Bangladeshi accounts and were on the cusp of accomplishing a similar feat in

Vietnam before authorities stumbled onto their plans. Access to even this most secure of systems had proven relatively simple. Get into the bank's system, obtain valid operator credentials, send fraudulent messages changing account postings, and establish a means of withdrawing purloined cash—usually employing ATM machines.

ODIN, the Qatari defense minister would later learn, had even bigger plans.

He was not going to simply deny service or steal money. His malware directed *all transactions* intended for Tehran's central bank flow into Riyadh's coffers—thereby launching a fiscal war with Sunni-Shia overtones. The clerics running Iran were going to be busy defending national security, national pride and religious purity. The ploy was a distraction, nothing that could not be undone, but it would serve Aboud's purpose. What ODIN needed was the machines, power supply and internet connections necessary to launch his coders' chaos.

It all sat 30 feet beneath the ground in Hadithah—unbeknownst to Amman, Riyadh or Washington.

Doha had purchased and supplied a sea of laptops, three servers, a generator and four microwave towers in Step One. Step Two consisted of constructing a bunker and overhead facility that would not draw American attention. Step Three was recruitment of skilled operators. Amazing what an endless supply of cash can accomplish, even in a shithole like Hadithah. ODIN was about to be surrounded by Indian IT operatives, Russian technicians and wayward Americans who proclaimed an alliance to Anonymous, an international coalition of anarchist hackers.

But first he needed to survive this drive across an open desert. A feat the defense minister appeared little inclined to abet. Any ridge or *wadi*, no matter how minor, was justification to slow and creep forward. On the fifth iteration of this "game," ODIN pulled out a 9mm and took aim at the defense minister's head.

"Do that again and I'll blow your brains out and leave your corpse to the dogs. Understood?"

"Sir," the defense minister was now whining, "I was merely trying to prevent our being ambushed."

"You drive, I'll worry about an ambush." A short retort.

Gas pedal went back to cutting a crease in the Toyota's floor mats.

ODIN lowered his gun and then did the unexpected, grabbed the steering wheel and veered so that they nearly rolled over. Pressed again the driver's door with a much larger American now sitting atop him, the defense minister squirmed in a desperate bid to reach the single-shot Derringer jammed inside a concealed pocket of his kakis. No joy, ODIN was already onto the ploy and nearly broke his arm as means of constraint.

"Out of the fucking truck." Not a request; that was an order.

Pistol to his head, the defense minister slid out the driver's side and lay on a bed of dry red talcum powder.

"Strip."

Not fond of being shot or dying, the Qatari disrobed to his underwear and piled all his belongings in front of a glowering former passenger. Who promptly soaked the lot in diesel from a jerry can fished out of the truck's back end.

"No, my personal possessions, wallet, phone."

Might as well have been pissing into the wind. ODIN dropped a match and watched the blaze reach through layers of sweat-stained khaki.

"Back in the truck, time for you to really drive."

A seemingly minor inconvenience, this burning of a man's clothes. Unless you are aware of developments in wearable communications technology. Using microchips and a weave of cotton and wiring, one could create a shirt that broadcast a person's activity levels and location, and even support internet connectivity for a smartphone. Pioneered in the latter half of the last decade, wearables now included hoodies that could text and baseball caps with a head-up display beamed onto a pair of the wearer's sunglasses. All developments closely monitored and employed within intelligence agencies around the globe.

ODIN's bonfire caused panic in a very dark room beneath head-quarters for Qatar's military intelligence directorate.

"We just lost contact with the defense minister."

Simple enough statement, but with blinding consequences for one of the Middle East's premier intelligence agencies. Doha was now flying blind.

As for the defense minister, he opted for an active verbal defense as a substitute for physical pacificity.

"You do not just burn an Arab man's clothes and then demand he travel through public places."

ODIN's response, "Shut up. We'll find you a man-dress in the next collection of Iraqi rednecks."

A less than polite way of suggesting the minister would be allowed a *dishdasha*—the long robe men favored across the Middle East be-cause it was cooler than tight-fitting Western clothes.

"I am insulted."

"Pull over, fuck head." ODIN's patience was visibly at an end.

Absent weapons, communications or any backup, the defense minister slowed to a halt.

"Out."

Allah was not on his side, this was seemingly nowhere in an unin-habited tract of southeast Iraq. He would dehydrate or die of exposure before anyone found him here.

"Drop the drawers."

The last insult, he was now standing naked before a Westerner.

"Back in and drive—without further commentary."

Thirty minutes before arriving at their destination, ODIN re-lented. Rather than risk ire with his behavior before a mission began, he directed they pull into one of the few compounds along this route. A wave of the 9mm won possession of a dingy dishdasha and the de-fense minister was once again clothed.

"Next time I shoot you." Not an idle threat.

"You are not worried about Iraqi roadblocks or security where we are going?" An honest question, phrased so as not to reveal his own concern about dying in a blaze of AK-47 fire.

"No," ODIN responded tersely. "There won't be any."

"You know where we are going within the town?"

"They'll find us."

This was exactly what the defense minister feared. *Who* would find them? And would it be the right side.

Needless worrying, Hadithah belonged to Aboud. Perceived traitors were beheaded before a mandatory crowd at the crossroads that marked the village center. Their welcome party was already waiting, in a battered Toyota Camry packed with explosives and set to detonate at any sign of trouble. Aboud took no chances.

Within 15 minutes they reached what Americans would loosely describe as "outskirts" to a village. Little more than a ramshackle collection of the same crappy construction they had passed during the past two hours.

The Camry and its coterie of armed occupants collected them in a suitable manner—by running into the Land Cruiser's rear end.

"What the fuck?" First explicative the defense minister had used during their entire trip.

"Stop the truck." ODIN had the 9mm palmed and pulled a sawed-off shotgun from a gym bag that had remained at his feet since climbing aboard. Unpleasant greeting for the first idiot to pass within 50 feet of its twin barrels.

A rear door on the Camry's right side opened slowly, a passenger emerged without weapon in hand. He simply gestured for them to follow and then climbed back into the Camry.

The Toyota slowly passed on the left and then wound its way into a neighborhood that had a compound complete with tin garage.

"Pull in." An instruction the minister expected, but was reluctant to follow. Death in a dusty, oil-splashed garage was not in his plans.

"Pull in, asshole, I don't want to draw attention from above." ODIN obtusely expressing concern about drone monitoring.

Absent any other choice, the minister followed instructions. Tin doors banged closed behind them.

"Get out, very slowly." It was the Camry driver's turn to be in command.

In the transition from daylight to dusk provided by a sealed garage, both ODIN and the Qatari had failed to note the presence of four jihadi standing amidst dusty shadows. There were no hugs, cheek kisses or handshakes. Just a gesture to follow the driver's lead. Down a narrow flight of steps.

And into a strikingly modern command post.

"Welcome." Aboud's Skype connection was projected on a 60-inch flat-screen mounted to a cement wall. Only his head was visible—a bit of vanity, despite the fact Aboud's physical condition was no secret.

"Allah be praised, you have made it without encounter."

The defense minister had other thoughts on that observation, but kept silent.

"You understand what we are asking?" Aboud was engaging in rhetorical nonsense. Of course ODIN knew why he was in Hadithah.

"This must all happen in the next six hours. We move forward at nightfall." As much operational planning as Aboud was ever going to divulge outside Baghdadi's inner circle.

ODIN simply nodded in the affirmative. If he could see Aboud, he was damn sure Aboud could see him. The defense minister knew NSA was sucking up every electronic emission—he figured the last thing ODIN wanted was to be voice-printed by some geek at Fort Meade.

"Begin immediately, this is now your home." Aboud's last comment before closing his Skype connection.

CHAPTER 18

AR-RAQQAH – 55 HOURS AFTER EMBASSY DETONATION

Hell hath no fury like a woman scorned, or a great power shamed. Al-Baghdadi watched as the citizens of Ar-Raqqah paid the price for his vision.

First to vanish were his two hospitals. Recipients of daily intelligence briefings, the American minions who decided where bombs should be dropped were well aware of his tendency to employ hospitals as command posts and shelter for senior personnel. A pair of cruise missiles obliterated Ar-Raqqah's hospitals less than 36 hours after Ambassador Dumpty's kingdom came to an inglorious end.

Next came the barrage of 500-pound JDAMs targeting schools and mosques. And then, only then, did the AC-130 gunship take up a lazy circle over the city, placidly destroying nondescript buildings that CIA assumed were billeting for jihadi fighters, and targeting anyone careless enough to be driving through the empty streets.

No mention of this campaign appeared on CNN or the BBC. Only *Al Jazeera* provided international coverage of the massacre. Coverage that inflamed the Sunni Arab world, while warming hearts and souls in Europe and the United States.

"Blast the bastards back to the Stone Age," was a common chant at gatherings in San Diego, New York City and Chicago. Politicians in Berlin, Paris and Washington were calling for his capture and trial before an international war crimes tribunal. Al-Baghdadi's intelligence assets warned him that Amman was now coordinating with Damascus, Jerusalem and Tehran in an unprecedented bit of solidarity intended to take "the head off the snake."

Well.

Residents of Ar-Raqqah were suffering; the inhabitants of Tel Aviv, Paris, London and Berlin would soon join them. The one difference, his subjects were acquainted with loss and largely inured to pain; populations residing in "civilized" cultures were not.

General Giulio Douhet was wrong, aerial bombardment did not demoralize a civilian population—rather, such actions coalesced support for existing regimes. The Americans and Russians were compelled to occupy Berlin as a means of suffocating Hitler and National Socialism. A lesson forgotten a generation later, as witnessed when Hanoi emerged triumphant after a quarter century of war despite Washington's endless strategic bombing campaigns. Similarly, Saddam Hussein sat atop Baghdad's political power structure even after a decade of harassment from U.S. economic embargoes, no-fly zones and occasional airstrikes. In each case, the citizenry did not revolt or decay into a weeping mass.

So let the Americans bomb.

What the Romans failed to realize was his requirement to acquire territory in order to remain legitimate. A caliphate, he was instructed as a graduate student, only remains viable so long as it continues to expand—a reflection of glories Prophet Mohammad had brought to this faith 1,500 years before al-Baghdadi's birth. Fail to expand and the caliph is just another failed Middle Eastern governor, leaving the *ummah* in poverty. He would have no such legacy.

Not that there was a rush to victory. A former caliphate spokesman had warned journalists, "We will conquer your Rome, break your crosses, and enslave your women. If we do not reach that time, then our children and grandchildren will reach it, and they will sell your sons as slaves." Heady stuff—material that al-Baghdadi had succeeded in propagandizing to over 100,000 youth of Islam. Allah be praised, the internet was a remarkable recruitment tool.

His was now a campaign of "offensive jihad," a transition from the defensive practices of ancient assassins and Yasser Arafat's bid for a Palestinian homeland. Roman bureaucrats decreed al-Baghdadi was nothing more than a terrorist. The jihadi knew better—this was a revolution. A revolution that ended in Baghdad, then Tehran, and on to Europe and Istanbul, where president-for-life Erdogan was busily undoing all the modern Turkish state's founder had fought to accomplish, thus becoming a direct threat.

In a sense al-Baghdadi knew he should not over worry about Erdogan. The Turkish military had demonstrated on more than one occasion a willingness to snuff out political bastards who overstepped an invisible secular/sectarian line. Erdogan only avoided a similar fate by playing the Kurdish card. Poking a sharp stick into Kurdish ambitions stirred a hornet's nest that subsequently kept generals busy striking back at the resultant attacks on Turkish sovereignty. Erdogan was a president who knew how to play one enemy against another, thereby creating operational space for his own ambitions.

What remained of Syria and Iraq bore witness to this competition between rival visions for Levant and Middle East futures. Al-Baghdadi promised a return to the true principles offered by a long-dead prophet. Erdogan sought to marry Sharia law with modernity—laying the foundation for a new empire. Al-Baghdadi played up the emotions of youth and ordered the slaughter of apostates and barbarians. Erdogan purchased influence using Saudi money and allowed for the murder of Kurds. His advantage was links to the European Union and NATO—al-Baghdadi only could lean on the Qataris and Aboud.

ANKARA – 55 HOURS AFTER EMBASSY DETONATION

Gunay's faith in his SWIFT team was rewarded less than 12 hours after he finished berating the lot as "incompetent louts, who only earned a paycheck by showing up for work." Hardly the worst insult he had hurled over the years, but in this case it worked.

A junior member of the group tasked with breaking through the encryption managed to complete a task no other Turk had mastered. They were in! Until the next crypto change—which could come at any time. So began a mad dash to track cash transfers from the Middle East. Gunay's instructions were very explicit—he wanted "small" movements—amounts in the seven-figure range that landed in an account that was likely brand new.

They found five that matched this characteristic—one of which came from a Qatari bank known to be employed by the royal family. There was no means of identifying the recipient, but the amount suggested a person of considerable value. Why else move $7.5 million to a single signatory account?

Gunay could guess. He had started this miserable career as an analyst and subsequently paid enough informants and operatives over the years. Putting two and two together, that much cash meant a man capable of significant mayhem. Guns for hire earn nowhere near such a salary. The same could be said of informants. Cyber skills, on the other hand, were in high demand. Now the question was who? And what or who was the intended victim? Puzzles beyond the scope of Turkish intelligence assets, but perhaps not CIA's. He reached for the phone and speed-dialed his counterpart at Langley.

Always good to have friends in low places.

Just as Gunay could not let the Doha connection drop, Saeed was quietly touching base with his contacts in Iraq. The two faces—More and Faheem—kept flashing through his mind. Why were they in Iraq? A rescue operation seemed a waste of such talent.

He hit pay-dirt on phone call eight—a member of Grand Ayatollah Sadr's inner circle.

Cornering Gunay in his office, Saeed provided a back brief.

He took the time to start with basics—no telling what Gunay knew or had forgotten about the obscurities of Iraqi domestic politics.

Clerics, he began, be they Buddhist, Catholic, Jewish, Muslim, Protestant or Tibetan, need a pedigree. With the exception of the last category, that means an "academic" education in the faith one is professing. "Academic" is a loose term, as some faiths use scholarly texts far less strictly than others. But a religious education is a religious education, be it from a deified leader or PhD—once completed you are anointed with the title of seer.

That's why Muqtada al-Sadr fled to Iran in 2007—there was no such anointing to be acquired in his homeland. Persians would have to accomplish this mission.

Setting him up for a direct conflict with the Badr Boys.

The Badr Boys—aka the Badr Brigade—were a collection of educated Shia who'd escaped Saddam's prosecution. Parked in Iran, they fell under the wing of Tehran's Islamic Revolutionary Guard Corps—the Quds Force.

In Western terms, the Quds Force is best thought of as an equivalent to Hitler's Waffen-SS. Joining the ranks meant you had the demonstrated loyalty, a vetted family and zealous practice of faith. It also meant that when cards were dropped on the table, you died for the religious clerics running Tehran, not the supposedly elected political lot. What Saddam had refused to teach the Badr Boys, they learned from the Quds Force. Very quickly.

Saeed picked up the pace of his story, enough background.

Flash forward, Sadr's Mahdi Army runs head-long into the Badr Brigade outside Karbala—in the midst of a religious holiday. Fifty Shia are killed and Sadr finally sees the light. Some of the Mahdi Army members followed Sadr's orders, other units choose to operate independently—splitting his forces into the "noble" Mahdi Army and the "rogue" Mahdi Army.

Returning to Baghdad, Sadr opted to follow Hezbollah's model rather than Yasser Arafat's direction for the Palestine Liberation Organization. That is to say, he directed his political operatives to seek control of public services rather than security departments. That was left to the Badr Boys. At the top of their list, the Interior Ministry, which was far more inclined to plant bodies than trees. Sadr had chosen poorly—until Baghdadi appeared and the ISF proved incompetent.

Now the "noble" and "rouge" Mahdi Army were a set of assets even Badr could not ignore. Instead they became a trio of forces within an ugly alliance bound by a common enemy—anything Sunni. Without this collection of heavily armed thugs, Ramadi would still belong to the Caliphate. Without this alliance and its focus on the Islamic State, Assad would not still be atop what remained of Syria.

Here's where Saeed finally had to admit his foreknowledge of the Americans operating out of Jordan.

According to his source, Sadr's men some 20 hours ago had intercepted a small American convoy near An Nukhyab, a vital watering stop for pilgrims on the *haj* to Mecca. A rundown village of 4,000 that was disputed territory—claimed by the Sunni-led Al-Anbar province and Shia-dominated Karbala province. Al-Anbar won when Baghdadi's warriors took the town, but then became a Shia stronghold when Grand Ayatollah Sadr sent his forces in to reclaim a treasured pathway.

This information on vehicles headed through the Al-Abyad Wadi and An Nukhyab drew no small amount of attention. This convoy was simply the latest to be intercepted. With one major difference— the Shia militia were specifically instructed to ensure this convoy landed up in An Najaf—on Sadr's doorstep.

Thus, the aging Marine and hulking Army major who Saeed

distinctly remembered were brought before Grand Ayatollah Sadr. Quite unexpectedly, according to his source.

Sadr was no philosopher, but he did understand strategy as played within his domain. While Syria had become a messy confluence of American, Iranian, Lebanese, Qatari, Russian, Turkish and Saudi Arabian influence and military expenditure, Iraq was a relatively simply affair. Keep track of the Americans and Iranians—watch for the Kurds, and play nicely with obscure outsiders who might be of assistance.

At this point, Saeed told Gunay, his source had become quite detail-orienting, suggesting the informant was present and not providing second- or third-hand intelligence.

With three assistants parked at his side, Sadr had beckoned the Marine into the room. Sadr's first questions were focused on what had become of the Green Zone.

The Marine apparently knew nothing of the impending disaster on Route Irish, nor of the Rangers standing on BIAP, or the fate of retired Prime Minister Malaki.

Sadr, however, seemed to know something about his uninvited guests.

"Washington sends its best in hopes of rescuing its worst." In English no less. Saeed's source had been surprised; even he was not aware the Grand Ayatollah spoke English.

Sadr had gone on to declare, "You speak our tongue." Also in English, not a question, this was a statement of fact.

Sadr then dispensed with English and switched to Arabic. But only after warning those in the room that this guest was listening to their every word.

"I know why you are here. I know what you are tasked with accomplishing, and I know you have no love lost on the Sunni or Shia family. Another American assassin or murderer charged with reclaiming U.S. sheep regardless of cost to the Arab flock."

This insult apparently drew a rebuke from the American. "Any different than the militia standing outside your door?" The man spoke in a raspy voice—hard to hear his Arabic.

Sadr was supposedly quick to retort. "I will not debate ethics and morals with a soldier. You have none, just a commander whom you blindly obey."

Saeed's source claimed Sadr then stared the American down. Likely a boast to depict his boss in the best light.

"You want to succeed?" A question from Sadr.

"Yes." From the American—in English.

Saeed took a deep breath, hoping Gunay was still listening. Things get very interesting from here. Apparently Sadr was quite deliberate and willing to allow the Americans to proceed—with assistance.

"You will work with my men and tend to their souls, no death from the air for Shia willing to enable your plans." Sadr had remained in Arabic, but his reference to the drones could not be clearer.

"You will also ensure Shia warriors are not laid to waste by the Daesh thieves." (Daesh, is an adapted acronym of the Islamic State's Arabic name, *Dawlat al-Islamiyah f'al-Iraq w Belaad al-Sham*. The acronym is hardly accidental—as Sadr well knew—but rather is similar to another Arabic word, *das*, which means "to trample down" or "crush," a phrase Baghdadi had made clear he did not want associated with his territory.)

The American made no comment on this set of orders.

"You will also take pains to leave a trail of blood no Sunni can mistake for cowardice. Simple instructions that come with a blessing for the Mahdi Army to assist in your undertaking. Do you understand?" All in Arabic.

According to Saeed's source the American again replied with a simple "yes," in Arabic this time.

"Allah be with you." Meeting was over.

Gunay looked at Saeed for a moment. Obviously thinking.

"How long have you known this?"

"Thirty minutes." Saeed saw no need to explain why he had made the phone calls in the first place.

Gunay leaned forward. "Something wicked this way comes." Shakespeare. Saeed knew the boss was well read. This observation, however, left him shaken.

"The Americans have dispatched some of their best from Jordan and the Qatari are paying top dollar for American talent that could be headed for ISIS. Would you like to bet there is a connection—perhaps personal in this 'coincidence'?"

Saeed never bet with Gunay—he always lost. Gunay was not sitting behind that desk because the man was a fool or political puppet.

"Get your ass back in the dust, something very bad is about to happen." Gunay's final comment before walking out to once again query the SWIFT team.

CHAPTER 19

There comes a point in life when the decision to cut and run becomes wiser than stand and fight.

More was urging a tactical retreat, while the Ranger sergeant major bid for a hold-and-defend approach. Nothing more frustrating than weighing competing advice from two aged NCOs. More expressed no confidence in Sadr's militia, his counterpart was all optimism about the Rangers' ability to defend the Candids.

"Run now and we fucking demonstrate the ragheads' ability to dictate terms on a battlefield." The sergeant major's bid to add a strategic context that might steer tactical considerations.

"Die in place and we'll be remembered as the modern 7th Calvary." More's crass reference to Custer and rejoinder to this grizzled Army hooah idiot.

Faheem could not believe he was listening to this bullshit. "Get us the fuck out of here—NOW!" Simple enough statement, one he could count on More to execute. The Ranger sergeant major would be dealt with later.

As the senior officer on site—a lieutenant colonel dispatched with the Rangers had suffered a compound fracture of his left femur during the initial paradrop and was now huddled in an Il-76, high on morphine—Faheem could at best muster the firepower of 120 men.

Oh, they were well-trained, experienced and understood a need to conserve ammunition. What they could not do was call upon artillery nor request close air support that might threaten damage to the runway or the Russian trash haulers that might be their only escape.

All considerations to be weighed even as mortar shells dropped in from the west and random technicals loaded with RPG-equipped jihadi probed their defenses from north and south. More's JTAC was now little more than a conduit for contact with an orbiting AWACS.

In an environment where the U.S. enjoyed air superiority—complete mastery of the skies—AWACS was a glorified airport control tower. But in this morass, complete with Iranian, Russian, Syrian and Turkish fighters screaming over a battlefield, AWACS could do little more than help American pilots avoid mid-air collisions. Rendering the JTAC status equivalent to a disc jockey who can select records but not broadcast without asking for assistance from an "engineer," who was out of sight and certainly off mic.

"Do they at least have situational awareness over Route Irish?" Faheem's sarcastic request of the JTAC's link to AWACS.

"No." Abrupt reply, absent even his standard "Sir."

"So what the fuck do we get from these clowns?" Faheem running short of patience with the USAF desk jockeys.

"Air strike coordination if or when you request, Sir." Faheem silently noted the JTAC remembered who was in command. Normally the goddamn USAF NCOs thought they ran the show.

"Worthless, I'd give my right nut for a unit flying AH-1 Cobras." An Army officer's standard dismissal of the USAF contribution to modern warfare. Oh, the flyboys could put GPS-guided munitions on target, but add weather or any kind of adversity and they would be grounded—likely sitting around a flat-screen playing Halo. Cobra pilots, on the other hand, could look an enemy in the eye and create havoc where the ragheads arbitrarily congregated awaiting direction from Allah.

Just as this lament was about to translate into a string of aimless epitaphs, his phone rang. A Washington DC 202 prefix, shit.

"This is Major Faheem." Polite in combat, later he would berate himself for not just ignoring the call—who is polite in battle? Some panty-waist USAF officer.

"Major, standby, I have the deputy secretary on-line."

"What? Who?"

No answer, just a click as the flunky transferred his connection to the boss.

"Major Faheem?" A question, not rhetorical comment.

"Yes, that would be me." Faheem was now standing at attention; some Army habits and traditions had made the transition into modernity. Always show respect for senior civilian leadership.

"I've been in conversation with Ambassador Dumpty. Are you aware of his situation?" Disembodied voice with no hesitation to color his conversation with a thick veil of disdain.

"Yes and no." A quick response that would dodge a requirement for participating in congressional hearings should he survive the shit storm that was building around BIAP.

"Route Irish is closed and 400 Americans are likely dead or dying, with 4,600 more trapped at the embassy. What are your intentions?" A guilt play from over 5,000 miles away. What a son of a bitch; must never have served in the military.

"Was not aware of that, Sir." Faheem now knew he was being recorded. "We're doing our best to avoid being overrun here." Best defensive line he could muster, particularly as More and the sergeant major were now leaning in to capture snippets of his conversation.

"How do you intend to assist the ambassador? Hunkering down to cover your own ass does not sound like a plan of action."

Faheem nearly hit disconnect before regaining his composure.

"Sir, I take orders from my superior officers and leadership at the Department of Defense. I presume you're calling from the defense secretary's office?" A needless question, Faheem already knew from where the call originated.

"No, I represent the secretary of state." Snob response, intended to intimidate and impress.

"Sir, I recommend you contact SECDEF. Until I receive further guidance, my greatest concern is that we put no further Americans in danger and maintain control of this possible evacuation point." The lessons of Benghazi were passed along to every Army officer who was compelled to deal with State Department functionaries.

Faheem was fuming—at this stage of the game he would have handed his phone to a journalist and let the press eat this clown. No such luck, the press was absent, perhaps wise enough to avoid suicide.

Silence from the other side, then an abrupt end to their connection.

More appeared silently off his left shoulder. "Now what?" he rasped.

"We figure out how to get out of here before they get lucky and hit a plane or overrun the airfield." Faheem's broad sketch of an operational plan that lacked tactical details. "You two," he continued with a wave of his hand in the direction of More and the sergeant major, "need to figure out how we're gonna get outta here!"

Second time he had issued those orders, there would not be a third.

A burst of emotional energy even More had not expected. The sergeant major was used to this type of drama—what he called "typical officer panic" (TOP)—and took Faheem's shouting in stride.

"Roger that, Sir," and he was gone.

WASHINGTON DC – 57.5 HOURS AFTER EMBASSY DETONATION

"What do you mean State over-stepped its bounds?" Words a president hoped to never have to utter when conversing with members of his cabinet. He was already rattled by the latest situation room update. A loss of 4,600 American citizens? How? Who? Why? Answers he needed from the DNI before demanding a declaration of war from Congress.

Due diligence had come to the political world. Speechwriters were already in a mid-sentence scramble for tonight's unscheduled Oval Office address on national television. The president wanted to ensure some journalist was not going to derail his remarks with new data.

Then this tempest in a teapot boiled over. In Washington, Hollywood for ugly people, political power was dependent upon an ability to raise money, connections, discretion and loyalty. In about that order of priority. Loyalty was fungible, cash was a necessity. Now he was confronted with a squabble between two men—his secretary of state and secretary of defense—with a demonstrated ability to open the pocketbooks of mega donors, just as all hell was breaking loose in Baghdad. A bad day gone worse.

Deep breath.

"Your commanding officer in Baghdad told an assistant secretary of state to go pound sand?" An Oval Office question the Pentagon's boss was not about to answer in an affirmative manner.

"No, the major apparently expressed concern about putting even more lives at risk." Politically correct response from a man who could just glimpse the White House lawns from his office across the Potomac River.

"He tried to make clear with State that no further action could be taken until there was coordination with supporting forces." A lie, but one the president had no ability to fact check in the immediate future.

There was no time for this silliness. "Get in front of the press and make clear we are doing everything possible to rescue all endangered Americans."

"Yes, Mr. President."

End of this crisis, at least for the moment. His next closed door session with the Cabinet was going to be a lecture on lanes in the road. Who owned what. Not the first time State and Defense had squabbled and would not be the last.

He leaned over and pulled open a desk drawer. Not for booze, but for the secure telephone so carefully constructed into a prized bit of furniture. Pictures of the Oval Office never revealed its occupant's concessions to modernity—a laptop, three phones, and a gaggle of lines providing connections to secure communications or electricity. All carefully routed through a desk leg and down into the floor.

In this case he was on a secure line with four speed-dial options— the DNI, CIA's 24-hour watch, NSA's 24-hour watch, and the White House situation room. He started with CIA.

CIA watch directors are all taught a singular lesson on day one of their training: if the black phone at the right hand side of their desk rings, drop everything and answer. Presidents were considered the agency's most important customer.

Two rings and a very nervous voice was on the other end of the line.

"Yes, Mr. President."

"I need an immediate update on the situation in Baghdad." No reason for please or niceties, the CIA officers never expected such pleasantry—they were also instructed to keep answers short, factual and simple. But also to attribute blame where it might be appropriate.

"NSA reports communications intercepts from ISIS stating the embassy convoy has been destroyed, no body count in the intercepts. NGA's working expedited collection and exploitation. DIA has no on-site reporting. State informs us at least 4,600 Americans remain on the embassy compound and radiation levels are not subsiding. Finally, NSA is now indicating significant pickup in activity on ISIS tactical channels—the cell phone grid in Syria and western Iraq is working overtime."

The commander-in-chief hung up, glowering.

Goddamn George Bush got America stuck in the morass 16 years ago and no one had ever figured out how to completely escape. Now it was his mess, with a threat of losses surpassing the 4,425 American deaths suffered over eight years of war. He'd pay to push Bush the Second and his wheelchair off the family's pier at Kennebunkport.

HADITHAH, IRAQ – 58 HOURS AFTER EMBASSY DETONATION

ODIN and the defense minister were offered desk space and ports for a laptop. And then left alone to work. ODIN had immediately made it clear the defense minister could go make tea, he needed to focus.

No sooner was the Qatari off to brew hot water than ODIN was on Tor and into an email account employed at the rarest of moments. Few enough that it drew no attention at Fort Meade or in other intelligence circles.

Save one.

The Mossad.

His message, delivered to an account he knew belonged to a top-ranking Israeli intelligence officer, was short and obtuse—no need for explanation, all the details had been worked out during an encrypted phone conversation two days prior.

"1800."

That was it. A set of digits that did not accidently happen to coincide with launch of his software surprise for the Iranians—and, unbeknownst to anyone else in the room or elsewhere, Ankara. Two of the four major players in this squabble were about to encounter chaos. Tel Aviv had paid him dearly for leaking the start time for Tehran's woes—but even the Israelis knew nothing of his plans for Turkey.

A stroke of genius, adding Ankara to his intended victims. The Turks were rabid capitalists and a conduit for monies flowing out of central Asia—including, ironically, profits generated in Armenia. Anxious to avoid Russia's corrupt banking system, ODIN's targets were willing to suffer the indignity of paying Ankara for access to

SWIFT and banks that met EU audit standards. At least until 1800 this evening. Then funds would be dribbling into a plethora of accounts he owned in the Caribbean.

He made no expression upon hitting send, but rather returned to checking connections and pinging servers.

A silent profession. No snap of ammunition being loaded into magazines, no shuffle of gear being stowed in packs or parachutes being packed, no yelling between men working on pure adrenaline in anticipation of facing down death. The new soundtrack for war was that of a keyboard and quiet cursing from coders trying to bypass security firewalls.

The defense minister returned. The tea was warm and sweet.

"Grab your ass, the fun is about to begin."

The Qatari took a chair, sat facing a display quietly playing CNN, and waited. Praying for the first time in his memory.

RAMAT DAVID AIRBASE, ISRAEL – 58.15 HOURS AFTER EMBASSY DETONATION

Pilots on standby, weapons loaded, air refueling tankers already rolling to take off. No communications except hand signals from support crew working with radios that broadcast no further than 200 meters. A mission in planning for ten years. Training for eight years. Security clearances for everyone on the airfield, and pilots sworn to secrecy on pain of imprisoned families.

Air conditioning a fighter on the tarmac with cockpit open and pilot garbed in G suit is an impossible task. "Take a shower on return to base," was an inside joke. Twenty minutes awaiting takeoff meant sweating out a liter of water. Every drop was worth what they were about to accomplish. An end to Tehran's nuclear game plan.

The aging KC-707 tankers went first. Older than their pilots by a generation, Boeing's promise of a replacement never met delivery timelines or cost estimates. Like the B-52, the KC-707s were rebuilt and rebuilt until everything from the avionics to aluminum skin were modern replacements. The best one could offer is that the tail numbers and a bit of the spine were original.

An Israeli AWACS went next, followed by four pair of F-15s to serve as combat air patrol. Sentries for the lumbering 707s.

At 1745 the F-16s loaded with family pack fuel pods—one tank on each wing and a third directly centerline beneath fuselage—lifted off. Everything headed east, over Jordan and then a skim along the Iraqi-Saudi Arabian border. No communications, no radars, no country clearance for overflight.

Tel Aviv had done everything.

Except inform Washington.

BAGHDAD INTERNATIONAL AIRPORT – 58 HOURS AFTER EMBASSY DETONATION

Faheem took his ass chewing from Washington in silence. Delivered by a Special Operations colonel, the tone implied what could not be said on record. "You showed the State pricks enough ass to make them go whining to daddy. Now get the fuck back to your mission." The line went dead.

Little reassurance given a rapidly deteriorating situation. With the coming dusk, Sadr's militia were falling back and toward the Euphrates. Why die here, on Saddam's palace grounds, when Sadr City was a short drive to the east? In short order, the ranks of uniformed Iraqi military members also began to melt away. Mortar fire was picking up from both east and west. More and the Ranger sergeant major were earning overtime trying to maintain a defensive perimeter.

Still no word from the embassy.

Faheem made the decision no one who was not on the battlefield would ever fully understand. Sprinting out to the nearest Candid, he screamed at the drunken pilot:

"START YOUR ENGINES. WE LEAVE NOW!"

Engines spooling up conveyed the message to the other Candid pilots. With rear boarding ramps lowered to within 12 inches of the tarmac, the Candid crews began backing away from the terminals. All that remained was the mad dash by those on the ground running for a place onboard. "Thank god for air cover." Faheem's first praise for pilots in countless hours.

And then they were gone.

A passenger list of approximately 200 Americans, Malaki and his remaining entourage.

ISIS owned the battle space, Faheem's team could only cut and run. On a plane built in the former Soviet Union piloted by men who could not recall the last time they were completely sober.

Hell of an exit.

CHAPTER 20

Only strict ethicists and the insane go to war on an even battlefield.

At precisely 1800 hours, things really got interesting.

Suddenly blind, the Turkish air force had been first to flee for home. Rapidly followed by the Iranians, then the Russians ... and finally Americans. Not that the American pilots were denied navigation and deconfliction—AWACS remained in full command of its domain. The problem was all the other airframes hurdling through flight paths on blind trajectories.

There is nothing more frightening than fighter pilots of unknown skill levels trying to navigate back to base using an onboard compass and altimeter, directional systems discussed in flight school but never really employed in this day of GPS and ground controllers with a god's eye view of all airspace.

ODIN made that advantage disappear for the Iranians and Turks at 1800—just as the sun was setting and dust would once again obscure the horizon. Every pilot operating over ISIS-controlled territory knew bailout was a piss-poor option.

Reacting to a flash message from the NSA watch—"Iranian and Turkish air control grids down, status of air defense unknown," followed by an even more worrisome, "unknown large-scale air operations over Arabian Peninsula"—CENTCOM ordered all American military aircraft to clear the area.

Just as Faheem's team was scrambling on board the Candids.

Charging up the lead Candid's ramp, Faheem found the morphine-dosed Ranger lieutenant colonel, Malaki with entourage in tow, a dozen army troops, a pallet of luggage—complete with two of Maliki's praetorian guard parked atop, waving AK-47s at anyone who came too close—and all of his team. Except ...

"Anyone seen the gunny sergeant?" No head nods north and south, just east and west.

"Think he climbed on another bird, Sir." Best answer he was going to get.

No time for him. Faheem stumbled up to the cockpit, which reeked of vodka fumes. "Major," the Russian senior pilot slurred in English, "We leave now, hold on."

Not a request, it was a suggestion implying bad things were about to happen.

With all instruments labeled in Cyrillic, Faheem had no idea what warning lights were good news or tidings of evil waiting to occur. One of them must have implied the rear cargo ramp was closed, as the plane lurched to the left and he found himself staring down the runway and listening as four turbines spun to top speed—brakes still locked in place.

"We leave fast, less RPG threat." The lead pilot again.

Faheem would have asked about the trailing two planes, but it seemed unnecessary. This lot had clearly departed other airports in an equal hurry.

What he failed to anticipate was the sudden lurch forward and his own body slam into the cockpit's rear bulkhead. A less-than-graceful maneuver that earned a chuckle from the then-unemployed navigator.

Designed using purloined blueprints for a C-141 Starlifter—America's chief heavy cargo plane during Vietnam and then Desert Storm—the Candid shared its U.S. progenitor's unique characteristic of possessing the steepest climb path capable for an aircraft weighing in at just over 105 tons.

Everything and everyone not strapped down in the cargo bay was now sliding to the rear, ripping up clothing, scattering weapons and eliciting a good bit of angry vocabulary.

Epithets that only grew louder when the Candid, upon take off, suddenly banked left and headed over downtown Baghdad at something approaching 500 feet off the ground and rising.

"Missile threat and we must clear air for following plane." The pilot's explanation.

One of Faheem's engineering classes at West Point actually validated this latter comment. Large aircraft generate sufficient turbulence on takeoff to cause a closely following plane to lose lift and use of control surfaces. Rolling away from the runway would allow the second and then third Il-76 to leave more rapidly than conventional air controllers could permit.

Number two took a similar approach to departure. More was wise enough to cling to the back of a chair normally reserved for a flight engineer. No luxury of sitting in this case—the seat was a strap down point for crew valuables, including a backpack for three more bottles of vodka.

That left jet three. Looking out his forward cockpit windows, the pilot could see a sea of headlights bounding across the terrain separating runway one from runway two. Caliph Ibrahim's army had arrived. Releasing his brakes with turbines at full throttle, the Russian aircraft commander made his best attempt to clear the swarm and take to flight. He almost made it. With landing gear clipping vehicles racing to establish a barricade and a barrage of small arms fire peppering his fuselage, the old bird came off the ground and began the left bank—only to be struck by two RPGs.

Fifty-five American servicemen, four Russian aircrew, and one crusty Ranger sergeant major would be subjects of eulogies and military lectures on courage or tenacity.

CHAPTER 21

BAGHDAD, IRAQ – 64 HOURS AFTER EMBASSY DETONATION

There is, within each human soul, a place wherein the moral compass no longer points north. East, south and west, but no north. It is a blinding realization; truth is a relative concept and security can only be purchased.

Ambassador Dumpty was desperately seeking to shed cash sufficient for salvaging his physical hide. With little success. Oh, there was the taxi driver who braved a now-deserted security zone in search of jobs or the occasional truck operator, but none could guarantee safe passage. Nor would they stay long outside the gates. Rumors of poison or radiation had quickly made the rounds in city markets and mosques.

Aside from the elderly, who were pardoned for being deaf and defenseless, there was no excuse for a failure of self-preservation. The American herd milling about within his embassy compound certainly had no such excuse. They were simply rendered motionless by panic and lack of imagination. A pair of conditions that would have been further aggravated had the good ambassador spoken of their evacuation's absent options. The airport was too far away for him to hear or see the planes' departures. It was a phone call from Washington that made clear his less-fortunate future.

"No helicopters on the roof." A none-too-subtle reference to Saigon on 29 April 1975. Great pictures, the largest helicopter evacuation ever. But there was no such option for Baghdad, particularly with air control out in Iran and Turkey. All flight-capable birds on the sole aircraft carrier in the Persian Gulf were strapped down on deck. Any launch, should the skipper deem it necessary, was reserved for overhead security. And those pilots were briefed on a need to be completely self-sufficient.

Hell of a way to conduct a war in an age of watches that could track distance, pulse and weather ... to say nothing of time.

An ambassador without clothes—just like the proverbial emperor. A condition made only more frustrating by dint of the fact he represented the "fucking United States." Mightiest nation on earth laid low by some two-bit hacker and a collection of rabid religious fanatics. This sentiment was made all-too obvious in his emails back to Foggy Bottom. Hillary Clinton may have been able to hide her correspondence on a private server—all subsequent secretaries of state were not so fortunate. His caustic comments would be public record for generations to come.

That, and his observations on the dusty demise he was now confronting with a bottle of good scotch evaporating into a glass on his desk. Phone calls were of little solace. The trophy bride cursed his idiocy in accepting this appointment and then hung up. No tears from her end, just a concern the children would be afforded a nanny and private school should he not return.

"Never marry the young," he randomly advised his RSO. "They have no sense of sentiment or remorse—just a collective greed." Words of wisdom spoken eight years too late. She could care less and the RSO was already trying to determine his own means of escape. There was no time to contemplate marital bliss or discord.

At least the wind had stopped. Swirls of red dirt slowly collapsed into dust piles that read out isotopes like findings in craters on the Nellis Range nuclear testing grounds. Better to die of melanoma than slow-motion cancer. An option he could not select on the chart for ending life. The jihadi owned his fate, now it was just a matter of time—should they let the compound hunker down for what used to be known as "the duration."

TEHRAN, IRAN – 64 HOURS AFTER EMBASSY DETONATION

This was never supposed to happen. An evil worse than Jimmy Carter's failed hostage rescue fiasco in 1980. All bad things occur in April ... Lincoln's assassination, sinking of the Titanic, Hitler's birth, Saigon's fall, Operation Eagle Claw, Operation Iraqi Freedom, and the Boston Marathon bombings—to name but a few. Yet, there they were. A stunned watch floor staring at screens with closed camera feeds revealing the impossible. Demise of Iran's nuclear capability—live and unedited.

Give the Mossad credit. It took three years and multiple agents before coordinates for targeteers were delivered with complete confidence. A bunkered facility five miles east of Esfahan. Non-descript, never registered with American imagery analysts, but confirmed as the sole site of Iran's nuclear armory by a scientist who died during interrogation. This was a bit like killing bin Laden—politicians played a 60–40 percent card game and then opted for 60. They were right. Or so Washington's airborne collection systems would prove weeks later. The radiation plume spewing toward Heaven was evidence enough for Congress and the Knesset.

Tehran was a serpent milked of its poison, but not its teeth. Even a venomless snake can inflict damage to an intended victim. A bit of folklore Tel Aviv never forgot. Munitions not employed outside Esfahan were dropped on weapons depots at airfields supporting Iran's motley collection of aged F-14 and ancient Soviet airframes purloined from Saddam during the first Gulf War. There was no time nor option for striking known ballistic missile facilities. Defense against those weapons would depend upon accuracy, weather and the gods.

However, the Iranian stockpile just to the south of Tehran

remained … just as Baghdadi would have predicted. At least his play was still an option.

The hornet's nest ODIN had set free was already heading for a new home. Like the Americans who flew missions against Muammar Gadhafi in April 1986—there it was, April again—the Israeli pilots responsible for wreaking havoc on this day would go unnamed and their families relocated. Glory in war is a wonderful thing if the enemy does not subsequently hunt down and murder your children.

"How the fucking hell …?" The only semi sentence a senior Quds Corps officer could utter as the pictures slowly scrolled across monitors in Tehran's command center.

"Sir?" A verbal tug at his sleeve from one of his underlings. "It gets worse."

"How, how could it possible get worse?"

"The banks are reporting sudden stops in international transactions." This was a timid comment, but one with even more stopping power. Weapons can be rebuilt, financial disaster brings governments to their knees.

"*What?*"

"Our bank auditors are reporting all transactions on SWIFT are going to a destination controlled by the House of Saud."

"WHAT?" A nonsensical repeat, he knew what had been said, it was just too hard to believe.

"Sir, Riyadh is stealing from the people just as Tel Aviv rendered us blind."

"Awake the president and supreme leader, we are in for a rude dawn," the officer intoned with a confidence he did not feel. "And I suspect others will also rue the morning." A phrase stolen from Admiral Isoroku Yamamoto, who famously is said to have prophesied even as Pearl Harbor burned, "I fear all we have done is to awaken a sleeping giant, and fill him with a terrible resolve."

WASHINGTON – 64.5 HOURS AFTER EMBASSY DETONATION

"You are fucking kidding me."

Direct quote from the president of the United States upon reaching his situation room still dressed in pajamas.

"Get the fucking Israeli piss-ant leadership on line right now."

"Sir, we've tried. No response on any hotline. Including those at CIA."

"Silence or stupidity is no explanation for war when we have 5,000 Americans trapped in Baghdad. Get them on the fucking line." Presidential decorum thrown into the wind.

"Sir, Still no answer."

"Shut them fucking down. Immediately. Turn off the intelligence feed and order the goddamn carrier to intercept anything, *anything* coming across the Gulf."

"Sir, the Navy is grounded given communications problems in the Gulf."

"Not anymore, asshole. Get them in the air and force the fucking Israelis to squawk or we take out approaching airframes as unfriendly. See if that message gets the Jewish bastards to talk."

A White House directive sent via teletype and fax. Certain to be intercepted and understood within Tel Aviv's inner circles in very, very short order.

"Yes, Sir."

Teddy Roosevelt was right, speak softly and carry a big stick. Enough moccasin time in the woods, he was ready to swing the cudgel … even if it meant striking your close friend across a delicate forehead.

"Humor me, any word from the DNI?"

"No, Sir."

"Fucker's fired at dawn." Last words before returning to the upper quarters of Washington's most famous address. "Goddamn intel boys won't know until two days after the *New York Times* has published an insider's story. Seventy billion dollars a year all so that I can read yesterday's news tomorrow."

AL AHMADI, KUWAIT – 64.5 HOURS AFTER EMBASSY DETONATION

Kuwaiti security was driving circles around the first Candid before engines could be spun down. A dangerous stunt; the turbines were known for sucking in men and spitting out ground meat. Security patrols learned to buckle in and stay clear of intakes.

"Out, out, no weapons!" A singular demand from the sergeant charged with corralling these lumbering giants.

The Russians waved, held up hands to windows in the cockpit 25 feet above the circling jeeps and then revved the engines. No sense in walking 500 meters when there was a perfectly fine ramp less than 50 meters from the terminal. Security would move before being run over. An object lesson in might makes right.

Faheem was busy dialing contacts in DC and requesting direction on next steps. The Kuwaitis were annoying, but in a useful manner. He no longer had to sweat drunken pilots or landing in places where he was more likely to be hung than granted diplomatic immunity.

"I want off, as soon as possible." His only directions for the senior pilot.

"*Da*, boss." Simple enough response.

A response offered less than 20 seconds before the first Pentagon call came through, and 90 seconds before a second followed in rapid succession.

"Where the hell are you?" This was no welcome-home call.

"Kuwait."

"Where's the ambassador?

"Baghdad."

"Fuck you, and now fuck me."

End of a call from an office on the State Department's seventh floor.

Only important people had offices on the seventh floor in most American bureaucracies ... exceptions granted to the White House, Pentagon and Congress. In those institutions floor choice made no difference in pecking order. A GS-15 was still a GS-15, regardless of desk location.

His next call came from a senior colonel in the Special Operations team at the Pentagon.

"Where are you?"

"Kuwait."

"The embassy people?"

"Still in Iraq."

Click. Amazing how the digital kids managed to make phone calls sound like connections from days of old. Or perhaps that was a real rotary being dropped on a cradle. This was the Pentagon after all—a building where money went to be spent, technology turned into weapons, and modernity was forgotten in a mound of paperwork. The colonel may have indeed been using rotary dial, an implement children only knew from trips to a museum.

Faheem called More. If anyone had survived the carnage at BIAP, he would've.

"Lock down, the Kuwaitis are going to want to search-and-detain any weapon or radio we possess."

Click.

Fucking More.

Reasonable response. Time for another call. This time to an American embassy where dust was not blowing down the halls.

Took three minutes for State to patch him into the RSO in Kuwait City.

"I need diplomatic clearance for my team, 60 soldiers and a soon-to-be Iraqi expatriate with security detail." Less said on an open line the better off they might be.

"Done." Cooperative response. "Do not open aircraft doors until we have people on site."

A short explanation for truncating standard customs requirements and keeping foreign governments at bay. A sealed airframe remained sovereign territory until the hatches were breached—from inside or out. Then the plane became subject to legal stipulations as enforced upon whosoever tarmac it was located.

They had survived to fight another day. Everything else was just bureaucratic maneuver, paperwork explaining damages, lost lives, and contextual circumstances. More already knew this drill well Faheem figured.

FALLUJAH, IRAQ – 64.5 HOURS AFTER EMBASSY DETONATION

Genghis Khan and his horde swept off the Mongolian plains. Hitler rolled east over Poland's wheat fields, and Tommy Franks captured Baghdad by driving armor through Iraq's desert southwest. Aboud faced a less daunting task. At least logistically.

Staging in Fallujah, a city made infamous in April 2004 when four Blackwater contractors were ambushed, burned and then hung on a local bridge—the opening salvo of Iraq's endless civil war—the town had been devastated by U.S. Marines and then nearly leveled a decade later when Shia militia and Iraqi regulars tried to take it back from ISIS occupiers. Once home to almost 350,000 people, it was now a ghost city of less than 50,000 starving souls. Citizens who were too weak, poor or mentally stunted to flee for higher ground.

Perfect location for hiding a collection of ragtag trucks, dusty sedans, and 5,000 angry young people waiting to join a jihad that would liberate Baghdad. Living conditions had been miserable. Water and electricity were luxuries of a previous generation. But the drones stayed away and allied airstrikes were few and inaccurate. Hard to provide a precision strike when there is nothing precise to destroy.

From this slum Aboud launched his capture of Baghdad.

There was no grand ambition, simply reach the Euphrates banks on the west and then destroy bridges that might allow a predominately Shia east-bank citizenry to respond in kind. Half of the capital was a whole victory—at least as the story would be played in Western news media. All embassies and major government buildings were on the west bank—Sadr City and a collection of slums constituted everything to the east. No one would miss the slums—what Caliph Ibrahim would call theirs was property that mattered.

Forty-five miles. Forty-five miles across windswept desert, past fig orchards, through barren wheat fields and over irrigation trenches breached by rotten timbers or hand shoveled dams. All the while fearing a return of air strikes or drone death from above.

It did not come.

Aside from fleeing Russian cargo planes, the Baghdad International Airport had been deserted. There was no security to counter on Route Irish. Local inhabitants were all too happy in assisting with a breach for the damaged roadway. It was, in more than one sense, a modern blitzkrieg. Done without aircover, up-armored vehicles or uniforms. Warfare had finally graduated from the pageantry of Napoleon and Lord Nelson to the grim reality of Ho Chi Min and Fidel Castro.

A grim reality about to be visited upon the Emerald City's remaining inhabitants.

HADITHAH, IRAQ – 64.5 HOURS AFTER EMBASSY DETONATION

"Done." ODIN's sole vocal expression in six hours.

"You own Baghdad and now I leave."

An astounding comment coming from a man quite alone amongst armed 20-year-olds, all of whom were rapidly exchanging glances and sneering. The computer geek was going to flee? Dead, perhaps, but walk out the door? Not on his feet.

ODIN shot first. The young lady sitting immediately behind where he was working. Then he shot the two young men standing with AK-47s as impromptu security. That left an apparent commander and his rapidly fleeing guards. Round one went into a back—paralyzed for life—round two took out the commander's left knee. By his count there were still nine bullets in the magazine and no shortage of targets.

"Truck, running with driver outside." A directive even the poorest translator understood.

He scooped up the weeping commander under one arm and began a drag to the basement steps.

One more round went into a sixteen-year-old who was going to defend Sunni honor. A bitter end to opposition intended to exhibit the jihadi warrior class at its finest.

ODIN jumped into the Toyota pickup, gunned the engine and pointed the grille north, smiling.

The Emir would be royally pissed.

EPILOGUE

ANKARA - 76 HOURS AFTER EMBASSY DETONATION

Answers. Everyone wants answers. Who, what, when, where—and, worst of all, how? Gunay had just survived one of the worst bureaucratic grillings of his career. The president's office was not pleased with his lack of hard data—nor his inability to explain what had happened to the nation's air control system. He had tried his best, he honestly had.

He started the out-brief with findings from SWIFT and explained how the trail pointed to a likely American culprit. He confessed to the CIA call and that agency's response—ODIN. This meant nothing to President Erdogan or his staff, so Gunay spent 10 minutes going through everything Langley had provided on ODIN's background—including his known former employers and adversaries. Turns out CIA knew about More's running dispute with the cyber warrior. That bit of information he delegated to Saeed alone.

Never a fan of politicos or public interrogations, Saeed was tight-lipped and played his cards close to the vest. He laid out what they knew of More and Faheem, explained the Americans' meeting with Sadr and then walked through what Gunay had disclosed of More's encounter with ODIN in New York.

Erdogan was not impressed. "You two spend million upon million and this is the best you can offer?" No promotions, service awards or bonuses coming from this session.

"Where is this ODIN now?"

Shoulder shrugs from Gunay and Saeed. However, Gunay did volunteer that his communications specialists had an intercept of the Qatari defense minister pleading for assistance in escaping from Iraq and ISIS. This was the best he could offer as definitive evidence Doha was involved in the whole mess.

Erdogan did not ask why, he already understood the Qatari Emir's motivations. Politicians inherently recognize a power grab, no matter how subtle.

Two hours after arriving the two men were dismissed from Erdogan's presence.

Gunay demanded Saeed drop him off at Fikriye's apartment—after he fished a bottle of Johnny Walker Blue Label out of the Mercedes trunk.

Saeed drove home, expecting another bleary demand for his driving services tomorrow, which promised to be unpleasant. But for now there was a break in the chaos. Gunay could go wallow in the muck. Saeed would purify himself with a long run through the mountains at dawn.

HEADQUARTERS U.S. 5TH FLEET, BAHRAIN – 76 HOURS AFTER EMBASSY DETONATION

Faheem sweated through a new set of ACUs before the 5th Fleet commander started asking questions. This brief had not gone well from the outset. No four-star commander likes to discover there is a unit operating in his area of responsibility after the fact. Faheem knew there would be ugly phone calls between Bahrain and the Pentagon within 15 minutes of his departure from this conference room.

Then there was explaining their meeting with Sadr and a promise to keep American airpower away from the Mahdi militia.

"You said what?" An incredulous tone in the admiral's voice suggested caution was an appropriate course of action.

"We—" He was unable to finish the sentence before he began. The admiral cut him off.

"We?" Simple question.

"Sergeant More and I." Faheem's answer.

"So, you and a Marine sergeant cut a deal with the most important man in the Shia world, without consulting with Washington or this command?" Not really a question.

"Yes, Sir."

"Ever dawn on you that such action was much above your authority? To say nothing of the political ramifications?" That was sort of a question—but more of a demand for apology.

"No, Sir, but I was acting in haste with American lives in peril."

"And that brings us to those American lives. You come home with 200 survivors and call that a victory?" The admiral was on a roll.

"No, Sir. It was the best we could do without endangering everyone who made it to BIAP."

"And," (the "ands" were going to be the death of Faheem at this point) "you bring me that asshole Malaki plus a bevy of his straphangers. Why, Major, *why?*" A pissed off admiral steaming ahead at full speed.

"Malaki provided the buses and gave us a link to Shia militia aligned with the Badr Brigade." At least Faheem had a logical answer for that one.

"What do you propose I do with him? A serious query from the admiral.

Faheem was tempted to declare, "Send him home," but figured that would only draw another verbal lashing. "Dispatch him to Iran?"

"Major, do you know what just happened to the Iranians?"

"No, Sir."

"Our good friends, the Israelis, just destroyed their nuclear stockpiles—or at least the known stockpiles. Tehran is not talking to Washington and sure as shit is not in communication with this command."

All news to Faheem. Should have turned on CNN in his hotel room before attending this meeting.

"Major, I am stuck with that son of a bitch and a batch of irradiated Americans. You and your Marine are worse than a plague of locusts. Get out of my fucking sight while we try to figure out a way to clean up your mess."

Dismissed—fucking More didn't even have to appear. Faheem bet that absence came at Langley's request. Friends in low places with influence.

Faheem needed a few in his own corner.

AR-RAQQAH – 76 HOURS AFTER EMBASSY DETONATION

A moment of quiet. Nothing falling from the sky, no artillery fire in the background, no gunshots on the streets. It would not last, the Americans were coming back. But for the moment peace settled over his capital. Al-Baghdadi sat and listened. A man atop his kingdom.

His plans for Tehran on hold. The damn Israelis had Tehran on high alert. There was little chance of success at this point. Aboud's nuclear ambitions would have to be put on hold. Perhaps for six months, but not forever.

Meanwhile he was silently celebrating the fact that Baghdad would soon be an addition to his caliphate. The Shia might be able to hold territory east of the Euphrates, for a short time. Soon his jihadi warriors would drive even those apostates south and out of sight. Let Sadr handle the refugees—with any luck, one of them would assassinate the Grand Ayatollah.

Silence, relish the silence.

BAGHDAD – 76 HOURS AFTER EMBASSY DETONATION

No one ever said life would be fair or conclude with a slumber upon a Swedish mattress promising good posture and an end to back or leg pain. Life often culminates in an ugly manner. Various needles and tubes inserted through veins, hands clutched to chest, drooling on your chest, or run down by opiates a doctor promised would cure— only to become an addiction that stole loved ones and then breath itself.

Ambassador Dumpty and his remaining subordinates—some 4,600 in total—provided Washington staffers clustered around their secure monitors a spectacle as horrific as it was timeless. Simultaneously broadcast on YouTube, instantly going viral for the ages.

The feed came via an encrypted connection through a handheld cell phone, which seemed to have unlimited battery life as row after row of 4,600 U.S. embassy staffers were marched to the edge of a newly-dug trench and mowed down with machine guns. Rising above the killing ground were half a dozen strands of barbed wire strung between three utility poles, festooned with various parts of the late ambassador. Dumpty's severed head was impaled atop the center pole, to which the cameraman returned repeatedly between groups of victims.

Someone in the group clustered beneath the situation room GOD managed the only words to be captured by in-place recorders for the next hour.

"How could this have happened?"

Ashes to ashes, dust to dust.

GLOSSARY

AC-130 – Tactical transport aircraft known as Hercules, but when converted to gunship has been called a Spectre, Spooky, Ghostrider and now Stinger. Cargo bay has been converted to gun platform featuring 105mm and 40mm cannons, backed up with 25mm Gatling guns.

AK-47 – 7.62mm assault rifle. First produced in the Soviet Union in 1945, the AK-47 is said to be the most widely distributed gun ever manufactured (74 million weapons). Comes with 5-,10-, 20-, 30- and 40-round magazines. Can also be outfitted with drum magazines holding 75 or 100 rounds.

AWACS – Airborne early warning and control aircraft. Derived from the Boeing 707, it provides all-weather surveillance, command, control and communications, and is used by the United States Air Force, NATO, Royal Air Force, French Air Force and Royal Saudi Air Force.

B-52 – Grandfather of the USAF inventory—the Stratofortress is a long-range, subsonic, jet-powered strategic bomber. In use since the 1950s, the bomber is capable of carrying up to 70,000 pounds of weapons and has a typical combat range of more than 8,800 miles.

Beretta 92FS – 9mm semi-automatic pistol used for law enforcement, military and self-defense. Manufactured under license elsewhere with different names. The Turkish version is a Yavuz 16.

BIAP – Baghdad International Airport.

C-4 – "Plastic" explosive—has multiple applications, including IEDs.

C-17 – Tactical and strategic transport aircraft known as the Globemaster. Replaced the C-141 in the USAF inventory. Can be used for heavy lift, troop transport and paradrop. Construction provides for armored cockpit and an ability to land on unpaved airfields.

C-141 – Called the Starlifter, the C-141 was a strategic airlift platform that went into service with the USAF in 1963 and was finally retired in 2006. Featured four of the eight engines used to power a B-52.

CIA – Central Intelligence Agency—headquartered in Northern Virginia; does not reveal number of employees or operating locations.

Claymore – An anti-personnel "mine" that is planted above ground with an explosive charge facing an adversary. Detonation causes the Claymore to spray 700 1/8-inch steel balls.

Dark Web – World Wide Web content that exists on dark nets, overlay networks which use the public internet but which require specific software, configurations or authorization to access.

EP-3 – Signals reconnaissance version of the P-3 Orion, operated by the United States Navy.

F/A-18 Super Hornet – Multi-role twin-engine fighter/bomber primarily launched off of aircraft carriers. Assigned to U.S. Navy and Marine Corps.

F-4 – The Phantom—a twin-engine, twin-seat fighter/bomber; was designed for employment on aircraft carriers and conventional landing fields. Heavily employed during the Vietnam War, the F-4 was phased out of the USAF inventory in 1995, but remains in service in other national air forces across the planet.

F-14 – Known as the Tomcat, the F-14 is an American supersonic, twin-engine, two-seater, variable-sweep-wing fighter aircraft. This was a favorite with the U.S. Navy.

F-16 Fighting Falcon – Single-engine jet fighter assigned to the United States Air Force.

F-15 Strike Eagle – Two-seat variant of the F-15 fighter. The Strike Eagle is primarily a ground-attack platform, but can be used for air-to-air engagements. Assigned to the United States Air Force.

GPS – Global Positioning System—employs a constellation of 32 satellites; provides user location data accurate within about 12 inches of precise position.

Human Terrain Mapping – United States Army program that used social science disciplines—anthropology, linguistics, political science and sociology—to provide military commanders and staff with an understanding of the local population. Widely employed in Afghanistan, less so in Iraq.

HUMVEE – U.S. military's modern version of the WWII Jeep. Capable of speeds approaching 60 mph. Were heavily up-armored after Iraq deteriorated into a domestic insurgency in 2005.

IED – Improvised Explosive Device—Came to the fore in Afghanistan and Iraq. The Iranians are rumored to have developed the "shaped" or Explosively Formed Penetrator for IEDs—when the device is detonated it punches a "lid" into a projectile capable of penetrating the up-armored Humvee's outer shell.

Il-76 – Soviet version of the C-141, called the Candid. Built to withstand poor maintenance standards and routine overloading, the Il-76 has remained a favorite among crews shipping illicit cargoes in Africa and throughout central Asia. Most of the aircraft are now well past design-specified total flight hours.

M1A1 Abrams – U.S. Army's main battle tank—weighs in at 54 tons. Main armament is a 120mm smoothbore gun, powered by a turbine engine generating over 1,500 horsepower.

M-16 – Standard issue 5.56mm rifle for U.S. ground forces. Can be manually selected to fire semi-automatic or full automatic (machine gun). Can be issued with a 20- or 30-round magazine.

M-4 – 5.56mm rifle, replacing the M-16 in U.S. military units. Can be fired in semi- or full automatic. Features a 30-round magazine and many have been fitted out with bore scopes including infrared target identifiers.

NSA – National Security Agency—Focused on electronic surveillance including communications and signals (any type of electronic emitter). Said to employ the greatest number of PhD mathematicians of any industry in the United States.

PDB – President's Daily Brief—Assembled from reports generated across the U.S. intelligence community. The PDB "belongs" to the director of National Intelligence, but is primarily written at CIA. Typically is limited to 20–30 pages a day.

QRF – Quick Reaction Force—Military unit, usually platoon-sized (15–50 personnel) capable of responding to a developing situation within 10–20 minutes.

RSO – Regional Security Officer—Principal security attaché and advisor to the ambassador at American embassies and consulates. Employed by the Department of State as special agents, a RSO is also the senior law enforcement representative at a U.S. embassy.

SATCOM – Satellite communications.

Stinger – Shoulder-fired ground-to-air antiaircraft missile.

SWIFT – Society for Worldwide Interbank Financial Telecommunication. The primary means by which over 9,000 financial
institutions across the planet conduct transactions—in the old
days, wire transfers.

Tor – Free software for enabling anonymous communication.
The name is derived from an acronym for the original software
project name "The Onion Router." Tor directs internet traffic
through a free, worldwide, volunteer network consisting of more
than 7,000 relays to conceal a user's location and activity from
anyone conducting network surveillance or traffic analysis.

ACKNOWLEDGEMENTS

Writing has frequently been described as a frustrating, lonely experience that often produces more scrap paper than finished text. Perhaps I have been sitting in front of computers for too long. While I find the creative process mentally taxing, transcribing thoughts onto paper is psychologically rewarding—after all, the only one I am arguing with is me. I usually win those debates ... usually.

In this case, I have been blessed to have a counterpart who keeps me honest, knows the art of putting pen to paper, and spins great yarns. Adam Dunn has pushed *Osiris* forward from day one and contributed no small number of characters, edits and ideas. Speaking from some experience, I can safely contend he is a master of this craft and deserves the highest praise one can offer. Thank you Adam.

As for content, I have to thank my counterparts in the U.S. military and intelligence community. Retiring after 24 years of serving to protect American national security, it is safe to say I have had the privilege of working for and with an outstanding cadre of quiet professionals. A collection of dedicated men and women, they deserve acclaim and recognition for accomplishments that rarely make the news. But, oh the stories we have shared over a drink and good meal—even if the combination was simply a cold bottle of water and lukewarm hotdog on a picnic table outside Baghdad.

Closer to home, I want to thank the people who kept me scribbling when other options were available. (Did I mention the sailboat or motorcycle?) Donald Pruefer is a life-long friend who continually reminds me to keep pressing forward on the latest project—his sense of humor and steadfast loyalty hopefully show through in this story. Steve Park kept the wolves at bay while I was engaged elsewhere. And Rich Cimino was always willing to weigh-in with thoughts ... even if our political perspectives were on different paths in the universe.

Finally, but certainly not last, I want to thank my parents. They have been an inspiration that kept me pounding a keyboard when other options were certainly more tempting. I have the good fortune of exchanging my thoughts and time with two educators who unselfishly share their insights and wisdom. There is no phrase that appropriately captures the level of appreciation I have for the opportunities they have provided over the last five decades of my quest to fill the bottomless bucket list.

A NOTE ABOUT THE TITLE

Osiris was a central god in the ancient Egyptian pantheon, within the circle of Isis (his wife), Horus (their son), and Set (his brother and murderer). Osiris is typically identified as the lord of the afterworld (i.e., the dead), but also representing transition, regeneration and resurrection. He is classically depicted as having green skin, a partially embalmed lower body, and bearing the trappings of power: a crown with two large ostrich feathers at either side; and the crook and flail, twin scepters symbolizing supreme rule.

A NOTE ABOUT THE AUTHOR

ERIC C. ANDERSON is a retired member of the U.S. Intelligence Community who served tours of duty in Hawaii, Iraq, Japan, Korea, Saudi Arabia and Washington DC. A former academic, he taught at the University of Missouri, University of Maryland, the Air Force Academy and National Intelligence University. During his career he produced over 600 articles for the President's Daily Brief, National Intelligence Council, International Security Advisory Board and the Department of Defense. In addition, he is the author of *Take the Money and Run: Sovereign Wealth Funds and the Demise of American Prosperity, China Restored: The Middle Kingdom Looks Forward to 2020, Adopting Ainsley: There's No Place for a Car Seat on a Motorcycle,* and *Sinophobia: The Huawei Story.* A life-long sailor and motorcycle rider, he claims to have spent endless hours on boats and put over 300,000 miles on a variety of Harley Davidsons.

A NOTE ABOUT THE TYPE

This book is set in Adobe Garamond,™ a font family based upon the typefaces first created by the famed French printer Clause Garamond in the sixteenth century, with its italics influences by his assistant Robert Granjon. Adobe Garamond was created by Robert Slimbach and released by Adobe in 1989.